"Well," Noah drawled, trailing a finger from her cheek down to her lips.

"There's just friends, and there's making love, and there's a whole lot of space in between. Maybe we can play it by ear, and find our way down the middle?"

Mollie shivered, fighting the urge to lean into him. She needed to get this straight. She was in uncharted waters and didn't want to run aground on some hidden reef. "So you're saying we'd be...what? Dating? And then what?"

He sobered. "And then I leave. But I've got until the end of the week, and I'd like to spend it with you. And I don't want to be fighting the urge to kiss you the whole time."

So, this was it. She could take what he was offering for now, and then he'd be gone. Or she could say goodbye to him now, and never see him again. Put that way, it really wasn't even a choice. "So are you going to kiss me again, or what?"

* * *

PARADISE ANIMAL CLINIC:
Let the love—and fur-ever families—fly!

D0448434

Dear Reader

Welcome back to Paradise! This is the third book in the series, and finally Mollie is getting her own happily-ever-after! I'm pretty sure she thought she was going to be spared such a fate—she certainly never intended to fall in love. But she does admit to a habit of taking in strays, and that is exactly what Noah James reminds her of when she finds him on the steps of the historic Sandpiper Inn.

Poor Noah had a little too much to drink on the plane to Paradise, but I think we can forgive him. He's flying solo on what should have been his honeymoon and feeling a bit sorry for himself. If that scenario sounds familiar, it's probably because it's the basis for the song "Drunk on a Plane" by Dierks Bentley. I'm a huge country music fan, and the first time I heard the song I knew there was a story hiding in those lyrics, waiting to be told. The idea wouldn't leave me alone...what would it be like to have your whole world turned upside down? What if being left at the altar wasn't an ending, but merely the start to a whole new adventure?

This wasn't an easy book for me to write, partly because both the characters are artists and I am definitely not, but the characters grabbed hold of me from the beginning, and I hope you enjoy their story.

Happy reading!

Katie Meyer

PS: I love to connect with my readers. Follow me on Facebook and Twitter, send me an email or check out my website!

katiemeyerbooks.com
Facebook.com/katiemeyerbooks
Twitter.com/ktgrok
katiemeyerbooks@gmail.com

Do You Take This Daddy?

Katie Meyer

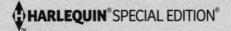

HARLEQUIN®SPECIAL EDITION®

Recycling programs
for this product may
not exist in your area

ISBN-13: 978-0-373-65959-3

Do You Take This Daddy?

Copyright © 2016 by Katie Meyer

Printed in U.S.A.

® www.Harlequin.c

Katie Meyer is a Florida native with a firm belief in happy endings. A former veterinary technician and dog trainer, she now spends her days homeschooling her children, writing and snuggling with her pets. Her guilty pleasures include good chocolate, *Downton Abbey* and cheap champagne. Preferably all at once. She looks to her parents' whirlwind romance and her own happy marriage for her romantic inspiration.

Books by Katie Meyer

Harlequin Special Edition

Paradise Animal Clinic

A Valentine for the Veterinarian
The Puppy Proposal

This book is dedicated to

My husband, for the countless weekends
he took kid duty so I could write.
(And for never mentioning all the book purchases
that show up on our bank statement.)

A big thank-you also to the Romance Divas
and all my writing friends who helped me
wrangle this book into submission.

And as always, my gratitude goes to my agent,
editors and the entire Harlequin team.
I couldn't do it without them.

Chapter One

It definitely wasn't the worst honeymoon on record, Noah James decided. That honor belonged to the unhappily married couple behind him, who had already argued about everything from who got the window seat to what where to make dinner reservations when they landed. Sure, he might be flying solo on the way to what should have been his honeymoon, but there were some good points of being jilted practically at the altar. Like two weeks in Paradise, Florida, stretching out in front of him, with no one to answer to other than himself. Unlike the newlyweds in the next row, he could eat when he wanted, go where he wanted, and do his own thing.

It wasn't as if his heart had been broken, although his ego had taken a pretty good beating. Dating Angela had been a mistake from the beginning. But breaking up with her wasn't an option, not after she'd shown him the test with the two pink lines. In that instant, his stomach had dropped and his world had turned upside down. Just like that, Angela went from a fling to a fiancée. She might not have been what he'd hoped for in a bride, but there was no way he was going to miss out on raising his child.

He'd been there to hear the heartbeat, chugging along. He'd squinted at the ultrasound pictures, unable to understand any of it but overwhelmed all the same. And he'd been there to feel the first kicks, the first tiny movements of his unborn son. Except it hadn't been his son at all.

Two days ago, Angela had disappeared, leaving her ring and a note after helping herself to a good portion of his available cash. Her written apology had been brief, as if she'd eaten the last cookie rather than torn apart his life. Some other guy was the father-to-be, and he'd been nothing but an easy mark for yet another gold digger.

He probably should have been embarrassed, but more than anything he just felt empty inside. Not that he missed Angela. The spoiled socialite had seemed fun at first, but her true colors had eventually come out and he was nothing but grateful to have avoided being legally bound to her. But losing his son, or what he thought was his son, had left him aimless and confused.

Finding out it was too late to get refunds on anything had given him the excuse he needed to get out of town, and away from prying eyes. He'd turned what should have been their honeymoon into a bachelor's vacation. He'd get his head on straight and come back to Atlanta ready to focus on his work. His art had suffered during the constant storm of his relationship, and it was time to recommit to it, while the name Noah James still meant something in the art world. Otherwise he'd have an ex-career to go with his ex-fiancée.

"Sir, would you care for a cocktail?" The flight attendant waited expectantly, a bevy of liquor bottles and mixers on her cart.

"I don't think so. Water will be fine." He'd never been a drinker, and ten thousand feet in the air seemed like a poor place to take up the practice. The pretty attendant started to hand him a plastic bottle, but had to move aside to let a mother carrying a fussy baby past. The child stared at him with big blue eyes while chewing intently on a drool covered fist, and Noah's gut clenched.

"I'm so sorry," the frazzled mother apologized. "He's teething, and walking the aisles is the only thing that seems to calm him."

Noah forced a smile. "It's fine." He even waved at the little guy as the mom turned to go back the way she came, and was rewarded with a gummy grin that cut right to his heart, stirring up the pain he'd tried to bury.

Maybe he'd have that cocktail after all. "Miss, could you switch that to a whiskey and coke?"

Noah meant to have one drink, just to take the edge off. He certainly hadn't planned on getting drunk. But seeing that baby had reminded him a bit too much of the mess his life had turned into, and before he knew it he had an impressive collection of tiny liquor bottles covering his seat tray. Which meant he was most definitely drunk. Or whatever came after that. Snookered? Wasn't that what the British called it? He was pretty sure he'd heard that on *Sherlock* once. Whatever you wanted to call it, it felt pretty amazing. The only problem was he was finding it just a wee bit difficult to walk. Also, he'd planned on renting a car while at the airport, but driving was most definitely out of the question. Luckily, a very nice security guard had been on hand to pour him into a cab.

Now that car was stopped in a gravel driveway fronting a three-story wood-framed building. Hanging from the wraparound porch was a sign, identifying it as the historic Sandpiper Inn. The perfect location for a destination wedding or honeymoon, at least according to the brochure he'd memorized. Hopefully it was also a decent place to sleep off a binge.

The driver unloaded Noah's suitcase from the trunk, and happily accepted the crush of bills he gave him for a tip. It was probably too much, but he was in no shape to do the math, and it wasn't like money was an issue.

No, his issues were far more complicated.

The most pressing being the way the ground kept shifting under his feet. Clutching his bag, he tried to navigate the wide, whitewashed stairs leading to the front door.

Tried, and failed.

Two steps up, and he was on his butt. At least, with all the liquid courage he'd imbibed, it didn't hurt. In fact, everything felt a bit numb. Maybe he should just

stay put until he sobered up a bit. He'd planned on relaxing and might as well start now.

"Hey, are you all right down there?"

He looked around. No one. Man, was he starting to
hallucinate?

"Do you need some help?"

This time, he managed to focus his not-so-steady
vision in the direction of the voice. Up on the porch,
sitting on a cushioned bench, was the most amazing
woman he'd ever seen. She had short, close-cropped
brown hair framing an elfin face. Her large brown eyes
were too big for the rest of her, and were currently ze-
roed in on him, and his not-so-stable perch on the steps.

"You're gorgeous." Oops. He was pretty sure he just
said that out loud.

Her laugh confirmed that yes, he had. Stupid alcohol.

"Are you drunk?" She stood up and started down the
stairs towards him. Her legs were long and lean, sprin-
kled with the same freckles that dotted her nose. She
stopped beside him, and he nearly toppled over trying
to look directly up at her.

"Could you not be so tall?" he asked, politely, he
thought.

"Sure." She chuckled again and sat down on the steps
next to him. "You are drunk, aren't you?"

"I guess so." He might as well admit it. "See, the
thing is, I don't drink."

She eyed him skeptically. "Right."

"I mean, I don't normally drink. But today I did. A
lot, I think."

"Yeah, I think that's a safe guess." She smirked.

"Well, you'll sober up, I imagine, but you can't do it here. Jillian sent me to keep an eye out for some guests who booked the honeymoon suite, so she could give them a special welcome. And I don't think a drunk guy collapsed on the steps is quite the welcome she had in mind."

"No worries," he reassured her. "That's me. I'm the couple you're looking for." He stuck out a hand for her to shake. She took it, eyeing him curiously. "Noah James."

"Mollie Post, nice to meet you." She looked past him onto the path below. "But where's your wife? Is she taking a walk on the beach or something?"

"She's not coming." The buzz must be wearing off, because that sounded pathetic even to him.

"What do you mean, she's not coming? You can't have a honeymoon without the bride."

She probably thought he was confused because of the whole drunk thing. But on this particular point he was perfectly clear. "Then call this a first. No bride. No wedding, for that matter. She took off before the rehearsal dinner." The pleasant numbness from earlier was replaced by a pounding in his head.

Her mouth dropped open. "Wow, that sucks."

Her frank acknowledgment did more than all the softly worded platitudes he'd heard in the past week. "Yeah, it does suck. But I figured it could suck back home, where everyone kept asking me if I was okay every two minutes. Or it could suck here, on the beach, with a margarita in my hand." His stomach lurched. "Although, I think I'll skip the margaritas."

* * *

Mollie watched the newcomer with fascination. She didn't care much for alcohol herself, but she wasn't bothered by his blatant drunkenness. He seemed harmless enough, and Nic and Jillian were right inside. Besides, he looked like he needed a friend. So she sat on the sun warmed steps with him, watching a flock of white ibises pick their way across the lawn.

He was certainly nice enough to look at, a long, lean body and slightly curly brown hair that was just a shade too long. His face was almost beautiful, with high cheekbones. But it was his eyes that really got to her, dark and hooded; they were the kind of eyes that saw things other people didn't. The eyes of an old soul, her Granny would have said. She wondered what his story was.

"You're staring."

"So? You're interesting to look at."

He blinked, and then let out a hoot of laughter. "Do you always say just what you're thinking?"

"Pretty much. I'm told I have no filter." She shrugged. "I tried, for a while, to learn to say the right things. But it never really stuck."

"I'm glad it didn't. Not many people are willing, or able, to be that honest. It's a good thing."

"Most people don't think so. My fifth grade catechism teacher found it particularly upsetting." She winked conspiratorially. "She smelled funny."

He winced. "You told her that?"

"I thought she'd want to know. Turns out, not so

much. People are funny that way. Most of the time, they don't want the truth."

"Yeah, well sometimes the truth is painful." He stretched, sprawling his lanky legs in front of him.

"Oops. Sorry. Yeah, I guess you've had your share of truth for the time being, huh?"

"You have no idea."

"So tell me." She stood up. "We can get some dinner, get you some water to flush out the booze, and you can tell me how you ended up on your non-honeymoon." Gossip usually wasn't her thing, but he looked like he could use someone to talk to. And she never had been able to turn her back on a stray.

His boyish grin was a startling contrast to his soulful eyes. "Did you just ask me out on a date?"

She hadn't, had she? "No, I don't date. But I'm hungry, you need to eat something to soak up the rest of the alcohol and I want to hear your story. New friends having dinner, not a date."

"You don't date at all?" He squinted at her, as if he expected to see some kind of physical sign to explain her celibacy.

"It's a long story, and I'm starving. Ask me again later."

"Shouldn't I get checked in first?"

"That depends. Can you make it up the steps yet?"

He looked up and shook his head. "Good point. Dinner it is. Where's your car?"

She wasn't one to let common sense interfere with an adventure, but even she had limits. "No car—we're going to walk. There's a place just down the beach path." A popular place for an evening stroll, with plenty of people around just in case her instincts about him were wrong.

"Afraid to be alone with me?"

Caution was part of it. Her parents might think she was naive, but she knew not to get into a car with someone she'd just met, even if she was the one driving. But there was another, more pressing reason.

"I'm just afraid you might puke in my car."

Noah would have laughed, but she looked pretty serious. And who could blame her? Luckily, he wasn't feeling nauseated, just weak and dehydrated. And more than a little foolish. He couldn't remember the last time he'd had more than a single beer. And yet he here was, too messed up to drive, being led around like a child. In other circumstances, he would have been humiliated. But even after seeing him at his weakest, Mollie hadn't given him a hard time. Sure, she'd laughed at him, but in a teasing way that had him laughing along with her.

She'd walked down those steps and treated him like a friend, not a stranger. He'd grown up always being the new kid, and even as an adult he usually felt like an outsider. His art had opened some doors, but having new money wasn't the same as fitting in. If anything, he felt even more awkward now, shoved into a rarified world, than he had when he was an army brat, bouncing from place to place. People might be more polite to his face now that he'd made something of himself, but celebrity hadn't bought him any true friends. Being welcomed and accepted right off the bat, that was something new.

They walked for about fifteen minutes along a gravel path that started behind the Sandpiper and ran alongside the dunes, and although they'd passed plenty of other walkers he hadn't seen anything that looked like a restaurant. "Where are you taking me, anyway?"

She winked. "Afraid I'm going to kidnap you?"

"Afraid, no. Hoping, yes."

She grinned. "Sorry, no such luck. But how do you feel about Cuban food?"

"I don't think I've ever tried it, but I'm hungry enough to eat anything." His stomach growled as if to emphasize his point.

"Well, then, you're in luck. We're almost there."

Another minute of walking brought them to their destination, which was more of a roadside stand than a real restaurant. A simple wooden structure, the walls were covered in a brightly colored mural, except for right above the order window where a menu board advertised the specials. There were a few tables scattered in front, topped with brightly colored umbrellas, and wafting on the breeze was the most amazing smell. "I think I'm about to start drooling."

She smiled. "Best Cuban food for miles, and coffee that will make you think you've died and gone to heaven."

Looking at her had him thinking he was already there. She'd blown him away from the beginning and it wasn't a case of beer goggles. In fact, the more he sobered up, the better she looked. She was tiny, at least eight inches shorter than his own six feet, with a slender, birdlike build. But it was her face that captivated him, the bone structure so fine it looked like she'd been sculpted by an artist's hand.

"I'll have the *ropa vieja*, and he needs a *medianoche* with a side of *maduros*. Oh, and a colada and a bottle of water." The man behind the window nodded, writing down the order.

He nudged her to the side, and got out his wallet. "Let me buy, please."

She motioned him forward. "Be my guest."

He paid what seemed like way too little and accepted a bag stuffed with food and the bottle of water in exchange. Mollie grabbed a full Styrofoam cup and two smaller, empty plastic ones. They picked a table farther back from the path and sat down facing each other.

'Okay, so tell me what I just paid for."

"My company?" At his pointed look, she took pity on him and started opening packages. "I got the *ropa vieja*. It's shredded beef, and it comes with rice. Your *medianoche* is a pork sandwich on a soft, sweet bread." She unwrapped it for him while she talked. "The name means midnight, because it's usually eaten when you are out partying and drinking. I figured it would be perfect for soaking up the last of the alcohol. The *maduros* are fried sweet plantains, and the colada is kind of like espresso, but with sugar."

Coffee sounded amazing. He reached for it, only to have her block him, putting her hand over the cup.

"First some food and water, then coffee."

"Anyone ever tell you you're kind of bossy?"

"All the time." She dug into her food, closing her eyes in bliss. "This is so good. How's your sandwich?"

He took an experimental bite. The salty pork and pickles vied with the cheese and mustard for top billing in his mouth. "Amazing." He took another bite, considering. "The bread's a bit like the challah my grandmother used to make. I like it."

"Challah? Are you Jewish, then?"

"My *bubbe* was, and my mom. My dad's Catholic. One item on a long list of things they disagreed on. I'm the only person I know that had to go to both confirmation classes and Hebrew school. Religion was just one more way to fight with each other without actually getting divorced."

"Wow. That's kind of crazy." She snagged another plantain from the bag. "The weirdest thing my parents ever did was putting up the Christmas tree the day before Thanksgiving one year, instead of the day after."

"They sound very…sane."

"If by sane, you mean utterly normal and conforming, yes. I'm definitely the black sheep of the family."

"That sounds better than the constant fighting at my house. Maybe we should trade."

Finishing his sandwich, he tentatively tried one of the plantains. Slightly crisp on the outside, soft on the inside, and sweeter than he'd expected. He quickly grabbed another before Mollie could finish off the container.

When he couldn't fit in another bite, he stretched and looked around. The haze of his earlier imbibing was gone, and he realized that although the restaurant itself was modest, the scenery was spectacular. Dunes stretched for what seemed like miles, and beyond them he could see the deep blue of the ocean. Sprawling trees dotted the landscape, with huge green leaves the size of dinner plates. "What are those trees with the giant leaves? The ones growing right in the sand?"

"They're called sea grapes. Those big leaves help block any light from the town that might disturb nesting sea turtles. In the summer they grow these berries that look almost like grapes that the birds go nuts for. And of course the roots help stabilize the dunes, so they don't just blow away." She poured coffee into the two small cups. "It's beautiful, but there's a lot of strength there, too."

Somehow, he had a feeling the same could be said about her.

Mollie wasn't blind; she'd noticed the way he looked at her. She just wasn't sure what to do about it. She should probably just walk him back to the Sandpiper, then go home and clean her house or something. That would be the practical thing to do. Of course, as the black sheep of he family, practical wasn't really her speed. Despite her mother's best efforts to the contrary. No, Mollie believed in going with her gut, and her gut was saying it was way to early to say good night. "How do you feel about a swim?"

He looked down at his faded T-shirt and jeans. "Now? I'm not exactly dressed for it."

"Not here, back at the Sandpiper. I'm assuming you packed a bathing suit?"

He grinned. "What, no skinny-dipping on the first date?"

Oh, boy. He was cute and he had a sense of humor. And was totally on the rebound. She was in deep trouble. But in for a penny, in for a pound. "I'll take that as a yes. I've got one in the car, so while you get checked in I can duck into Jillian's room and change."

"Jillian?"

"Jillian Caruso. She and her husband, Nic, own the Sandpiper. They have a private suite on the first floor."

"Ah, when I made the reservations, Nic mentioned he'd gotten married recently." He stood and collected their trash, disposing of it in the labeled bin. "I don't think I would want to live where I worked, with the public just a few doors away all the time."

"Yeah, it's not ideal. But they're building a separate house on the property, so they can have some privacy. Plus, with the baby coming, they'll need the space."

His smile faded at the mention of a child.

"What, don't you like kids?"

"Actually, I do. Up until a few days ago, I thought I was having one."

She sat back down on the picnic bench. "Excuse me?"

He rubbed a hand across the stubble on his jaw. "My ex-fiancée is pregnant—she's due in a month."

"But it's not your baby?"

He shook his head. "When she ran out on me, she left me a note. It said she couldn't go through with the wedding and that I shouldn't try to find her. Of course, she might have said that last part because of the money she took out of my account before she left." Shoving his hands in his pockets, he started back towards the Sandpiper. "She also admitted the baby wasn't mine."

Shell-shocked, Mollie just sat there for a minute, watching him walk away. Getting dumped was bad enough, but this was like something out of a daytime talk show. Belatedly getting to her feet, she ran to catch up with him.

What did you say after an admission like that? Maybe it was better not to say anything. He was a stranger and probably didn't need some random girl poking into his life. On the other hand, sometimes it was easier to talk about the hard things with someone you didn't know. And she wasn't good at keeping quiet anyway. "Do you believe her?"

He sighed, looking out over the water as if the answer to her question could be found along the horizon. "I don't know. I guess I have to. I don't even know where she went, and I don't know why she'd lie about it. Not that I understand much about why she did what she did. We never should have been together in the first place. She was a friend of a friend, no one I knew well, and it didn't take long to figure out we had nothing in common. But by then she was pregnant, and in the shock of it all I made a bad situation worse and proposed." A harsh laugh escaped. "It seemed like the honorable thing to do, you know? But the more I got to know her, the less I could picture us married. We spent the last several months living mostly separate lives. At least she had the guts to realize it wouldn't work. I was too stubborn to admit it."

"Because you thought she was pregnant with your child."

"Exactly. As much as I wasn't in love with her, I wanted to be there for my son." He stopped, and a hint of a smile touched his lips. "I was there when they did the ultrasound. It's a boy."

"So what do you do now?"

"There's not much I can do. I hired an investigator. If he finds her, I'll get a court order for a DNA test. But he doesn't sound very hopeful."

"That sucks."

He rubbed a hand through his hair, shoving it back in a burst of frustration. "Yeah, it does. But I couldn't just sit around my apartment, feeling sorry for myself. I was going to go crazy."

"So you came here."

He shrugged. "I still had the tickets and it was too late to get a refund."

She walked beside him in silence, feeling his betrayal and confusion. Maybe she'd only known him a couple of hours, but there had been an instant connection as soon as she'd seen him on the stairs at the inn. He was like a wild animal that'd been abused, beautiful and proud but hurting inside. She couldn't fix his life, but maybe she could help him forget a bit, at least while he was here. Sometimes a distraction was almost as good as a cure.

At the Sandpiper, she stopped in the gravel lot to retrieve her bathing suit. She unlocked the trunk and swung her backpack over her shoulder before taking the path to the front door.

"Does everyone in Florida keep an emergency bathing suit in their car? The way people up north keep blankets in theirs?"

"Not everyone. But I do, in case I want to go for a swim after work or on my lunch break."

Noah's single suitcase was on the covered porch where the cab driver had left it. He grabbed it with one hand and held the door for her with the other. "Wait, you go to the beach on your lunch break?"

"Sure, it's only five minutes from the clinic I work at. I can change, have a half-hour swim, then eat a sandwich in the car on the way back to work."

He shook his head and smiled. "No wonder they call this place Paradise."

Mollie left Noah at the front desk with Jillian while she went to change into her suit. Ducking into the master suite, she noticed the new hardwood flooring in the halls and fresh paint on the walls. Nic was doing a great job restoring the old inn. Of course, she was happy that Jillian had such an incredible place to live, but the whole idea of marriage and babies seemed so grown-up and responsible. She wasn't ready for all that yet. She'd seen what raising a family had done to her mother's dreams—her professional dance career had ended before it really began—and Mollie wasn't going to let that happen to her.

Which was why she didn't date. Dating led to relationships—first comes love, then comes marriage, then comes Mollie with a baby carriage. No, thank you.

She had things she wanted to accomplish, and getting sucked into the mommy track wasn't in the plans.

Jillian poked her head around the door. "Hey, I just checked in a Noah James. He said you two are heading to the beach?"

"Yeah, we're going to get in a swim before dark."

Jillian's eyebrows rose. "You know he was supposed to be here on his honeymoon, right? He's on the rebound, hard-core."

Mollie rolled her eyes. "I'm not sleeping with the guy—we're just going swimming. I found him on the front steps earlier, and we ended up getting a bite to eat at Rolando's. He seemed like he could use some cheering up." She reached back to adjust the tie of her bikini top, torn between sharing his story with her friend and protecting his privacy.

Jillian's expression softened. "Yeah, I guess he does. I don't know very much about him—he dealt with Nic when he made the reservations. They know each other, though, from some welding project he worked on for Caruso Hotels. Nic says he's a good guy, but still, be careful, okay? I know you never turn away a stray, but you don't want to get wrapped up in that level of drama."

Be careful. Safety first. Look before you leap. Why did everyone feel the need to say things like that to her? She was twenty-six, not twelve. She was getting tired of everyone she knew treating her like she couldn't handle herself just because she led her life a little differently. So what if she ate sushi for breakfast sometimes or preferred thrift-store T-shirts to business casual? And yeah, she had daydreamed and doodled her way through high school, but not everyone could be the straight-A student her sister was. She'd graduated just the same, and if her choice to focus on the arts rather than something practical was a risk, it was one she was willing to take. Her goal was to live life without regrets, to follow whatever adventure came along.

Maybe that's why she'd been so ready to take a chance and invite Noah to dinner. A small rebellion against all the caution signs surrounding her. Or maybe he was just that intriguing. Whatever it was, she wasn't backing off. Her gut told her he needed a friend right now, and despite what everyone seemed to think, her gut was usually right.

"We're going for a swim, not robbing a bank. I'll only be a stone's throw from your back door. Heck, you can send Nic to find us if we aren't back in a few hours." She threw the backpack on her shoulder and headed for the door.

"I might just do that." She grinned. "But in the meantime, he's lucky to have you to introduce him to Paradise Isle. He couldn't ask for a better tour guide."

"Well, when you've never been anywhere else, you get a good appreciation for a place." She shrugged. "But thanks. I'll see you later."

She found Noah waiting for her out back. Nothing like watching a man's mouth fall open to boost the ego. She didn't have the curves of a supermodel, but her new push-up bikini top seemed to be working just fine. "You can put your tongue back in your mouth now."

He chuckled. "I'll apologize for staring if you want, but it would be a lie."

She understood his predicament. She was doing some ogling herself, taking in all six-foot something of him. She'd known he was tall and broad-shouldered, but she hadn't anticipated all the lean, tanned muscles he'd been hiding under his street clothes. Jillian was right—this man was no stray.

"Shall we?" He gestured for her to pass, and she padded down the sandy wooden steps, the boards still warm from the heat of the day. Summer had barely started, but the temperatures were already in the eighties. At the bottom she paused for him to take off his shoes; she'd stashed hers in her backpack when she changed.

"You can just leave your shoes next to the steps. No one will touch them."

He didn't argue, and she gave him a mental bonus point. Not all guys tolerated being told what to do. The sand was hot under their feet, but when they neared the water it phased it out. "Just so you know, the water is still pretty cold this early in the year. By August it will be like bathwater, but for now it's a bit bracing." Then, grabbing his hand, she pulled him in with her.

"Whoa, you weren't kidding. This is freezing." He stopped her when they were about chest deep. Well, chest deep for her; he was significantly taller.

"You'll get used to it." She released his hand and leaned back to let herself float, her body rocked by the calm swells. Nothing was better than this. It was that magical time of evening when the day was over but night hadn't quite taken hold yet. The sky was an abstract ballet of colors dancing in the light, changing minute by minute as the sun dropped. If she had to be stuck in one place forever, Paradise Isle wasn't a bad choice. But she didn't plan on staying stuck.

Turning her head, she could see Noah floating beside her, as mesmerized by the view as she was. Moving on instinct, she reached out and took his hand, sucking in a breath at the buzz of attraction that sparked between them. She'd meant to show him a bit of the peace that Paradise had to offer. Instead, he was creating his own version of chaos in her world.

The cold Atlantic water had washed away the last lingering effects of the alcohol, leaving Noah feeling more clear-headed than he had in days. Maybe longer. Everything had gone haywire the minute he'd met Angela. At first her need for excitement had been fun, the constant parties a way to let loose after the months of work he'd put into his latest project. But then the drama started. Late-night fights over nothing, constant demands for attention. She thought that a man of his fame, who had been touted as one of Atlanta's most eligible bachelors, would live an extravagant life and spend lots of money, preferably on her. His modest lifestyle had been a shock, and any attraction had faded quickly, on both their parts. But the drama had lingered until the final day, with fights over everything from what car he drove to where they were going to live.

Mollie tugged at his hand. "You aren't brooding over there, are you?"

"Are you kidding? I'm literally in Paradise, hanging out with a beautiful woman, watching the sun set. What do I have to brood about?"

She blushed at his compliment, a faint pink creeping across her face. He liked that behind her boldness, there was an innocence about her, too. There was no cunning or guile with her. "How long have you lived here?"

"All my life," she answered easily. "Actually, I was born on the mainland, at Palmetto Hospital, but only because the Paradise Medical Center wasn't built yet. I've been an islander since I was a few days old."

"Seriously?" He couldn't imagine living in one place your whole life.

"Yeah, I'm a native. How about you—where are you from?"

He never knew how to answer that question. "Everywhere. Nowhere."

She stood, wiping at the water dripping down her face. "That's not an answer."

He stood, too, a full head above her. "I'm not trying to be evasive. I just don't have a good answer. I was born in Colorado, but I've lived in more places than I can remember. Dad's army, so we moved every few years. I think the longest I stayed in one place was four years, and that was in college."

She tilted her head, considering him with those big brown eyes that seemed to see more than they should. "Was it hard? Moving all the time?"

A dozen different goodbyes flashed through his head. "Yeah. It was hard."

She ran a hand up his arm, her fingers leaving a trail of saltwater and awareness. "I'm sorry." Her voice was as warm as her touch, drawing him in.

"Don't be. I had just as many hellos as goodbyes." He

moved closer until he could feel her slick skin pressed against him.

She tipped her chin up, her gaze locked on his. "Well then, I guess we could consider this a hello."

He could make a joke, laugh it off and swim back. He probably should. He hadn't so much as looked at another woman since he met Angela, even though they'd had separate bedrooms for the past six months. But there was a single drop of water clinging to Mollie's lip and he just had to have a taste.

Slowly, giving her time to stop him, he leaned down and pressed his lips to hers. She tasted of salt water and sweetness, like the taffy he'd had at a carnival as a kid. She floated in his arms as they kissed, the waves washing against them while he feasted on her mouth. He wanted more, to take her right there, to feel her from the inside out while the first stars of the night peaked through the sky.

Mollie pulled away, leaving him with her taste clinging to his lips. "This is crazy."

"It doesn't feel crazy." It felt incredible.

"Despite the fact that you're on the rebound and I don't date?"

"Well, yeah, aside from that. Are you sure you don't date?" She was pretty and fun and could have her pick of guys. So why was she off the market?

She nodded, bobbing in the water. "Very sure. No offense, but men have a way of getting in a woman's way when it comes to a career. I've got too much I want to do to risk getting distracted by a relationship."

She had a good point, but something in him wanted

to try to change her mind. Maybe it was the months of celibacy talking or the need to forget all the crazy parts of his life, at least for a few minutes. Whatever it was, he didn't want to say goodbye, not yet. "I don't know, distractions can be fun."

She shivered. The sun had fully set now, and the air was no longer warm enough to make up for the cold water. "Nice try, but I don't even know you."

"Sure you do. You know I'm a military brat, my parents are crazy, and I can't hold my liquor. What more is there?"

She splashed him. "I mean, I don't know where you live, what you do for a living, if you have any pets, that kind of thing."

"To be fair, I don't know any of that about you, either. But I'm willing to keep making out anyway." His body didn't care about any of that stuff. And the rest of him was too spellbound to think straight.

"How very generous of you." She was shivering again.

Taking her hand again, he waded up to the shore. He wrapped her in one of the soft, oversize towels they had left there and then rubbed himself down.

"You're like ice. We need to get you into some dry clothes."

She rolled her eyes. "One minute you're acting like you want me out of my clothes, the next you want me to put more on. I can't win with you."

"Very funny. Come on." He led the way to the steps and onto the deck, then held the door for her to go inside."

She hesitated. "I'm not going up to your room with you."

He hadn't expected she would. But he wasn't ready to let her walk out of his life yet, either. "Mollie—"

"No, wait, I've been thinking. You said you want to get your mind off things while you're here, right?"

"Yeah, I guess. But that doesn't mean I expect you to—"

She smacked him. "Get your mind out of the gutter. No, I was going to say, why don't you let me show you around while you're here, be your personal vacation guide?"

Was she serious? "What about your work, or whatever?" He didn't know what she did, but she must have some kind of responsibilities.

"I've actually already got the week off from school and work."

"School?" He'd thought she was in her midtwenties, just a bit younger than him.

She shrugged. "I take college classes at night, and I arranged my vacation hours at work to match up with the break between the fall and summer semesters. So I've got the time." She blinked those big eyes at him. "I'm not suggesting anything, well, romantic—I'm not looking for a relationship, and I don't do one-night stands. But I'd like to be your friend while you're here. If you're interested."

Interested in spending a week in Paradise in the company of a beautiful woman? "I can't think of anything I'd like better."

Mollie sipped her coffee and checked the kitschy black-and-white cat clock hanging on her living room wall. It was almost nine o'clock; Noah should be there any minute. As if on cue, she heard a car pull into the driveway. Nerves flopping in her stomach, she quickly smeared on some tinted lip gloss. Makeup so wasn't her thing, but after that kiss last night, soft lips seemed more of a priority than they had before. Not that she was planning to kiss him again. Still, better safe than sorry.

She opened the door before he could knock and was struck again by that feeling of awareness that had tickled her senses from the first time she saw him. It was a bit like the tingle before a lightning storm, a warning of the heat and power to come.

He was dressed casually, in a pair of cargo shorts and a gray army T-shirt, and had a bag from Sandcastle Bakery in his hand. "Ooh, breakfast?"

"If you consider a variety of sugary pastries breakfast, then yes. I had the cabdriver stop on the way here."

"That's the very best kind of breakfast. Let me get some plates." She led him into her tiny kitchen and handed him the plates. "Do you want coffee or orange juice?"

"As a Florida tourist, I think I'm required to at least try the orange juice."

"Good point." She poured a glass for him, and then motioned to the back door. "We can eat on the patio."

He reached the door before she did and started to open it, only to slam it closed again.

That was odd. "What are you doing?"

He swallowed hard. "This is going to sound crazy, but do you have bears around here?"

"What? No way. They see them over near Orlando

and Ocala, but we don't have bears on the island." A thought occurred to her. "Wait, you haven't been drinking again, have you?" If he had some kind of problem, she needed to know now.

"No, I'm telling you, there's something out there in the bushes. Something big."

Realization dawned. Oops.

"Yeah, about that..." She pushed past him and opened the door, letting out a whistle.

"Are you crazy?"

"Hey, I'm not the one seeing imaginary bears." She pointed and he peered around her. Out of the bushes came her large, but not quite bear-sized, dog.

"Holy cow, what is that? And why does he only have three legs?"

"That's Baby, and you be nice to him. He might be big, but he's sensitive."

Noah's eyes widened. "He's yours?"

"It's more that I'm his. But don't worry. He's a total sweetie. He just looks intimidating, right, boy?" The massive dog trotted over on and sniffed the bakery bag.

"If I give him the donuts, will it keep him from eating me?" To his credit, Noah hadn't retreated back into the house, but his color looked a bit pale.

"He's not going to eat you. And he's not allowed any donuts. He's on a diet."

"So you're saying he's hungry? Great. That's just great."

She shook her head. "I can't believe you're afraid of dogs."

"That's not a dog," he protested. "Beagles are dogs. Cocker spaniels are dogs. That's a—"

"Mastiff. An English mastiff, to be exact. And he wouldn't hurt a fly, so stop acting like he's the big bad wolf. You're going to hurt his feelings." She rubbed the big dog's head and took the pastries from Noah. Immediately, the dog left him and followed her, nosing hopefully at the bag. "I said no. You already had your breakfast, and Cassie says if you don't lose weight you're going to end up with arthritis. Go lie down."

Chastised, the oversize canine shambled off to lie in the grass. She put the bag on the bright blue picnic table and sat in one of the mismatched chairs. Noah cautiously joined her, keeping his attention on the now-snoozing beast. "So, what happened to his other leg? And who is Cassie, some kind of doggie-diet guru?"

"Cassie's my boss. She's a veterinarian. She and her father own the clinic I work at. As for Baby, a rescue group we work with brought him in when he was just a puppy. He'd been hit by a car over in Cocoa Beach and one of the volunteers found him. We fixed him up, and when no one claimed him I got to bring him home."

"So you work at a veterinary clinic? Are you some kind of animal nurse or something?"

She finished the bite of donut she was chewing. "No, that would be Jillian. She's the veterinary technician. I'm the receptionist. Oh, and I teach obedience classes on the weekends."

"Is that what you always wanted to do, work with animals?"

"Not as a career, no. I do like the dog-training part

of it—I don't want to give that up. But working in an office, any office, for the rest of my life would suffocate me eventually."

"Well, what are you going to school for?"

"I'm only going part-time, but I'm a photography major, much to my parents' disappointment." She grimaced. "They're glad I finally went back to school, but they think I should do something practical, like accounting."

"But that puts you right back in the office all day."

"Exactly."

"Okay, so forget them. What do you want to do?"

Right this second, what she wanted to do was to lick the powdered sugar off his lips. But that probably wasn't the answer he was looking for. "What I'd love to do is travel, take pictures, maybe work for a magazine. I want to make a name for myself as a nature photographer. But as my parents have repeatedly pointed out, art isn't exactly a practical career choice."

"Photography, huh? Can I see some of your pictures?"

She hesitated. She always felt so vulnerable, showing her work to a new person. And with him, for whatever reason, the nerves were multiplied.

"Please? You show me yours, I'll show you mine."

If that was a pickup line, it was awful. "Show me what?"

"My sculptures. Well, photos of them. I might have some on my phone of the most recent one, or you can just look it up online."

"Excuse me?" Sculpture. Her stomach dropped. Oh

no. He couldn't be. She pulled her cell phone out of her pocket and started frantically typing. At the top of the search results was Noah James, metal sculpture artist. She clicked on the link and there he was, in a photo taken at the grand opening of the Caruso Hotel in Las Vegas. Behind him was the sculpture the hotel had commissioned for the lobby, an abstract swirl of metal twining at least ten feet high.

She held the phone out and showed him the photo. "You made that? Jillian told me you were a welder!"

"I did make that, and I am a welder."

She shook her head in frustration. "No, you're not. I mean, I'm sure welding is involved, but you're one of the most famous metal artists in the country." Hadn't a celebrity magazine included him as one of its sexiest men alive last year? She remembered only because he'd been the only artist in a list of politicians, actors, and pop stars. But he'd had a beard then; no wonder she hadn't recognized him right away. That, and well, famous people didn't tend to show up in small towns like Paradise. She looked down at the screen again, trying to understand how the man sitting across from her could be the man in the article. "This says your last sculpture sold for almost a quarter of a million dollars! I thought you welded rebar for building foundations or something. Why didn't you tell me?" She tossed the phone down, and covered her face with her hands. "Oh my God, I made out with Noah James. *The* Noah James." Holy crap. Girls like her did not go around kissing famous millionaires. So much for him being a stray in need of a helping hand.

He reached over to pry her hands away. "I didn't tell you because it didn't matter. I'm still the same pathetic guy you found on the steps yesterday."

She rolled her eyes. "You might be the same guy, but from where I sit your bank account just got a lot bigger. For crying out loud, I fed you food from a roadside stand." She paused, considering. "Although, I will say, I feel better now about making you pay for dinner."

He hoped his financial status wasn't going to change things for her. He was happier here, eating donuts from a sack than he'd ever been at fancy galas or exhibitions. A few high-dollar sales hadn't changed who he was or what he wanted. And right now, he wanted to see her photos. He'd bet money she was better than she thought she was. Her house and garden reflected an innate understanding of color and light. Even her mismatched furniture showed an artistic flair. "So, are you going to show me some of your work, or not?"

She looked at him. "After finding out you're a famous artist? No way. My ego isn't ready for that kind of scrutiny, not this early in the morning."

Eager as he was, pressing her would probably do more harm than good. "Fine, then let's get started with whatever's first on the tour. What are we doing today? Swimming, Jet Skiing, sightseeing?"

She shook her head. "Nope, today we're fishing."

"You mean, with worms and stuff?" He hadn't been fishing in years, and had never really enjoyed it. Sitting on the edge of some muddy pond doing nothing for hours on end didn't sound like much fun. Of course, he'd never had her for company before.

"No worms. You'll have fun, guaranteed, or your money back."

"Easy to say when I'm not paying you anything anyway."

She winked. "Exactly. And if we want to actually catch anything, we need to hurry. Once it really heats up, the fish stop biting." She stood and gathered their breakfast remains. "Baby, come on. Time to go."

The big dog stood and shook himself, then loped over, panting and wagging his tail.

"He's going with us?"

"Oh yeah, he loves to fish. He goes nuts when he sees the poles. We can't leave him behind."

Of course not. That would be crazy. After all, who wouldn't want to spend their vacation fishing with a moose-sized three-legged dog? He eyeballed him again. "Does he even fit in the car?"

"Sure he does, but the longer we stand here talking about it, the less time we have to actually fish."

That had kind of been the point. But he'd asked her to give him the real island experience and if that meant fishing, well, then, he'd fish. Fishing with her would be better than doing pretty much anything without her. "By all means, let's go then."

She stacked the dishes in the sink, then came back out and locked the door. A small detached garage was beside the house, and she ducked into it, telling him to wait. A minute later she was back with two fishing poles, a long leash, a bulky camera bag and what must be a tackle box. Setting the box down, she snapped the leash on Baby and handed it to him. "You take him, I'll carry our gear."

He recognized the challenge in her suggestion, and took the leash. It wasn't like he was afraid of dogs. He'd just never met one that looked like it could eat him whole and still have room for dessert. Following Mollie around to the front of the house, he kept a tight hold on the leash and a close eye on the dog.

He had to admit, it was pretty impressive how well the dog managed on three legs. Unlike most people, he didn't seem to care that he wasn't quite perfect. He just was happy to be alive. When Noah stopped in the driveway beside Mollie's little hatchback, Baby moved closer, bumping Noah's hip with his massive head. Getting the hint, Noah gave the dog a cautious scratch and was rewarded with a tail wag forceful enough to knock over a small child.

Mollie secured the poles to a roof rack, and then took the leash and loaded the dog into the cargo area. Noah watched with fascination as Baby wedged himself into a comfortable position, then proceeded to shut his eyes as if the whole process had exhausted him. By the time Noah was buckled into the passenger seat, there were loud snores coming from the backseat.

Mollie started the car. "I still can't believe you're a famous artist."

"And I can't believe you're still thinking about that. I'm just me, and this is like any other fishing trip, okay? Just you, me and Baby. Which, by the way, is a ridiculous name for a hundred-pound dog."

"He's almost two hundred pounds, actually." She grinned. "I thought the name might help him seem less intimidating."

"It didn't work."

"Hey, I saw you petting him. Admit it, you like him."

"Fine, yes, I like him. What concerns me is how he feels about me."

She laughed. "I see your point. But you don't have to worry, you're pretty easy to like."

The drive to the marina was quiet, other than Baby's snoring. Inside her head, though, chaos reigned. Was she crazy to be spending more time with Noah? Safety wasn't her concern; between Baby and her years of martial arts training, she wasn't worried about him trying anything. But how could she keep things fun and casual when every minute around him had her liking him more? And not in a platonic, let's-be-friends way. Not even close. But even if she was willing to break her no-dating rule, in a few days he'd be headed back to his real life, and she wasn't interested in being someone's vacation fling. Not to mention he was on the rebound. No matter how she looked at it, anything other than friendship would just be asking to get hurt.

He broke the silence first. "Do you go fishing a lot?"

"Not as much as I'd like. Between work and school, it's hard to find the time. But I try to go out at least every few weeks, usually with my dad." Which reminded her—she really ought to make an effort to go see him and her mom while she was off this week. She made a mental note to call them as she turned into the parking lot of the marina. Boats of all sizes and shapes dotted the water, from beat-up fishing vessels to sleek yachts. There were quite a few houseboats, too, some that were bigger than her own home.

"What are those garage-like buildings?" Noah pointed to a row of open fronted warehouses where boats were stacked four high in individual slots.

"Those are dry racks. People pay to have their boats stored there to protect them from the elements. The marina uses a big forklift to move them in and out."

"Valet service for your boat?"

She smiled. "I've never heard it put quite that way, but yeah, basically." Getting out of the car, she checked that she had everything and let Baby out of the back. "Let's head up to the marina store. I want to get some bottled water and we're going to need bait."

"So what's the deal? Are we renting a boat here?"

"Nope, my Dad has one stored here. Well, I guess it's the family boat, but he and I are the only ones that take it out. My sister is a workaholic and doesn't make it down here much. And Mom likes to tag along, but she won't take it out by herself."

With Noah carrying the gear this time, she walked with Baby, waving at a few of the people down on the docks. They passed the restrooms and a covered picnic area, and then the pool.

Noah turned to take it all in. "I always thought a marina was like a parking lot for boats, but it almost seems like a campground or something."

"Well, it's kind of both. Most people just store their boats here, but some live off them. For them, this is a neighborhood of sorts. And even the day trippers some-times like to get a drink or something to eat at the res-taurant."

"I wonder what that's like, living on a boat."

"I've thought about trying it, but haven't had the guts or the money to actually do it." She shrugged her shoulders. "Maybe someday, though."

They reached the small bait-and-tackle store along the waterfront, and she reminded Baby to behave.

"You can bring the dog inside?"

"Everyone here knows Baby. They'd give me hell if I didn't bring him in." Once inside, she walked past the rows of shiny lures and the displays of custom-made rods to the coolers in the back. "You grab us some water and ice. I'll get the bait." She picked out a package of frozen shrimp and some squid. Usually she went with live bait, but given Noah's lackluster reaction to the idea of a fishing trip, the frozen stuff might be a better way to ease him into the experience.

Taking everything up to the register, she paid while Baby was fawned over by Frank, the owner. "How's my favorite pup?"

"She's doing great, thanks. How are you and Marie?"

"Oh, we're good." His smile crinkled the lines on his face. "The grandkids were down last week and about wore us out."

"And I'm sure you can't wait for them to come back again." The elderly couple doted on their grandchildren, and the feeling was mutual. The kids were often under-foot around the marina, enjoying the fresh air whenever they had a school break.

"You got that right." He tipped his head toward Noah, who was inspecting some handmade boat models. "Who's the fella?"

"Oh, he's one of Jillian and Nic's guests, someone Nic knows from work. I'm just showing him around a bit." In a small town like Paradise, it was better to stop any rumors before they started.

"Mmm-hmm. Well, you just make sure he treats you right. You never know with those tourist types. At least you've got Baby here to keep an eye on things."

She had no doubt the loyal dog would defend her from an attack, but what she really needed was protection from herself and the growing attraction she felt every time Noah was around. She wasn't about to explain that to Frank, though, so she just nodded and headed for the door.

"Hey, don't forget me," Noah called, putting down the replica sailboat he'd wandered over to.

Forget him? She hadn't stopped thinking about him since she saw him on the steps of the Sandpiper. No, the only thing she was in danger of forgetting was her common sense.

Noah followed Mollie out of the dimness of the bait shop, squinting against the harsh glare of the sun. Taking one of the plastic bags from her, he matched her pace down one of the long docks extending over the blue-green water. "Which boat is yours?"

She pointed to a midsize vessel about halfway down, a picture of an orange and the words *Main Squeeze* emblazoned on the hull.

"Cute name."

She rolled her eyes. "That was Dad's attempt to suck up to my mom. He was trying to get her to like the boat more."

"Did it work?"

"Nope. I mean, I'm sure she appreciated the gesture, but she'd rather stay on dry land and fuss with her plants. The garden is her happy place."

"And the water is yours?"

"One of them. I'm not real picky. Anywhere outside works for me."

"And anywhere you can snap off some good shots?" He nodded to the camera bag she'd pulled from the car, now hanging from her shoulder.

A quick smile of acknowledgment was replaced with a grimace as she stepped onto the deck, absorbing the movement of the sea like a seasoned sailor. "Someone must have left some bait on board." Her nose crinkled, her freckles bunching up as she made room for him to join her. "Sorry, I'll rinse out the bait wells if you'll keep an eye on Baby."

At the sound of his name, the dog stood up from where he'd been sprawled on the warm wood planks of the dock, leaping across the gap between the dock and boat with much more grace than Noah expected from the oversize amputee. "Show-off."

Switching the bags to his left hand, he braced his right on the post beside him and swung down, a bit more clumsily than the dog but without falling on his butt, thankfully. Being out of his element was one thing; making a fool of himself was another.

Baby sat calmly a few feet from his mistress, not needing any minding that Noah could see. Mollie had her back turned, a hose in her hand as she bent over the bait wells hidden inside a set of bench seats. He wasn't quite sure what she was doing, but he wasn't going to distract her as long as he had such a nice view. Long, tanned legs ended in a trim bottom with just the right amount of curves, displayed nicely in a ripped pair of cutoffs that had him looking at denim with new appreciation.

"There, that's better." Mollie stood up, tossing the short hose back onto the dock. Kicking off her flip flops, she stepped up onto the gunwale, stretching to reach the spigot sticking out from a mooring post.

"Careful!" His breath caught at the way she was leaning out so far over the edge—and not just because of the way her tank top was riding up.

Ignoring his warning, she turned the water off and then hung the hose up neatly on the hook next to it. "Relax. I'm not going to fall overboard. I promise."

As if to prove her point, she balanced for a minute, hands free, before hopping down beside him. "See, totally safe."

She might not be worried about drowning, but with her standing only inches away neither one of them was safe. She was close enough to taste, and he'd like nothing better than to kiss that cocky grin off her face. But she'd set the ground rules, and he wasn't enough of a jerk to break them. He hoped.

Backing up, he put some breathing room between them. "All right, so, what do we have to do now? Tell me how I can help, and don't say watch the dog—he obviously doesn't need a babysitter."

Amusement flashed in her eyes. "You caught on to that, huh?"

"That you were just giving me a job to salve my ego and keep me out of the way? Yeah."

Unrepentant, she shrugged a shoulder. "Well, I really didn't need you to do anything, and a lot of guys would get offended if I did everything myself and didn't let them help."

"Are you kidding? I'm on my vacation. Or honeymoon, whatever. I think my ego can handle sitting here and watching a pretty lady take care of things. But," he added, more seriously, "I'd love to learn, so maybe you can explain what you're doing, and then next time I really can be of some help."

"You've got a deal." She took the bags from him and dumped ice into a cooler located under yet another seat, stowed the drinks, and then put the frozen bags of bait in the now clean bait wells. "No ice on these. We want them to thaw a bit so we can use them. If we were using live bait, we could fill these compartments with seawater, and then turn on the air pump to keep the water oxygenated."

"So noted. Drinks and bait separate, and live bait should be kept live." He leaned his weight against the tall captain's chair, enjoying watching Mollie work. "So what's next?" She was an excellent teacher, and he was definitely an eager student.

"Next you get out of my seat so I can start the boat." She gave him a gentle nudge with her elbow, and even that contact was enough to have his body reacting in ways that were not particularly appropriate. Glad he'd worn baggy shorts, he eased past her, careful not to let their bodies touch.

She inserted a normal looking key attached to a bright orange foam keychain and the engine rumbled to life. "We'll let it idle for a bit while I text my dad our float plan. Then we'll untie the lines and be on our way."

"Float plan?"

"It's like a flight plan, but for boating. Whenever any of us go out, we let someone know when we are leaving, where we plan to go and when we should be back."

"That's smart of you." He relaxed a bit; he should have known she'd take the proper precautions. As impulsive as she claimed to be she also had a level head on her shoulders.

Mollie stared for a minute before seeming to accept his compliment at face value. "Thanks. All right, now, time to cast off. I'm going to untie this line, if you want to get the other one."

Pleased that she'd given him a job, no matter how small, he carefully unwound the rough rope from the anvil-shaped metal cleat bolted to the dock. As soon as he was done, Mollie pushed off, freeing the small craft from its moorings before returning to the captain's seat. A minute later they were slowly motoring out of the marina towards the Intracoastal Waterway.

Looking back at Mollie, a peaceful smile on her face, the breeze blowing her hair as she effortlessly steered the boat through the channel, he couldn't help but think it might not be just the fish in danger of being hooked.

* * *

Mollie focused on steering the boat down the center of the channel, pretending that whatever this feeling was that sparked around Noah was nothing more than the normal response to being around someone as famous as him. Of course, it, whatever it was, had started before she'd known his identity. Which would mean it was something else entirely, something more primitive, more basic.

She certainly felt more primal, more aware of her own body around him. Cutoffs and a tank top had never felt so revealing, not that he'd done or said anything inappropriate. He was sticking to the terms of her agreement, but that didn't stop the air from almost crackling when they touched. Not that she planned on touching him again, but the boat was only so big and casual contact was hard to avoid.

"What's that?" Noah broke into her musings, pointing to a large wooden platform perched atop a post at the water's edge.

"A nesting platform. The power company builds them for the osprey, to try to keep them from nesting on utility poles. If you keep an eye out, you should see a few with actual nests on them. The ospreys around here are a bit unusual in that they don't migrate, so the breeding season goes on all year."

"They live in Paradise, literally." He gestured out over the clear water towards the picturesque sandy shore. "I wouldn't want to migrate, either. What could be better than this?"

"Adventure? New things, new places, new people? Stores that stay open past nine p.m.?"

"Whoa, where did that come from?" Noah's eyes crinkled in concern, his lazy slouch against the railing belying the edge beneath his words. "I thought you loved this place. Isn't that why you're showing me around? So I can see how great it is?"

Mollie bit back a defensive retort; it wasn't Noah's fault she felt so conflicted. Taking a few deep breaths of the salty humid air, she tried again. "I do love it here. I can't imagine a better place to grow up, or anywhere else ever being home."

"But?" He raised an eyebrow, waiting for her to continue.

"But I want more!" She felt her cheeks heat at the outburst. Great, now she sounded like a spoiled brat. "That sounds awful, doesn't it?"

He grinned. "Not awful. Just sounds like you have a bit of wanderlust, that's all. Nothing wrong with wanting to travel a bit, strike out on your own."

"You get it." He put her rambling thoughts into words so easily it was like he could read her mind. "My family, my friends… They think I'm crazy to want to leave, I don't even have anywhere in particular I want to go. I guess I just don't want to end up tied down like my mom did."

Noah waited for her to explain, not pushing, but letting her know he was listening if she wanted to share. Funny how it was so much easier to talk about this stuff with a near-stranger than her friends.

"My mom was a dancer, a talented one. She had

a chance to go to New York and dance with a major company. I've seen the newspaper clippings, the old programs—she has a whole scrapbook full. She could have been famous."

"What happened?"

"She met my dad." And that had been the beginning of the end when it came to her mother's dancing career. "They fell in love, one thing led to another and a year later she had a ring, a mortgage and a baby. By the time I came along, she had given up on it completely. Once Dani and I were old enough for school, she started working at my father's law office as a secretary. She's never done anything else."

"Does she regret leaving dance?"

"She says she doesn't." Mollie shrugged. What else could she say? That she wished she'd never given up her career to have kids? Not exactly something you could tell your daughter. "She says she's happy, that having a family was always her real dream."

"But that's not what you want." It was a statement, not a question.

She shook her head. "I don't know if I ever will. I'm not like her. I can't even think about it. I want some adventure in my life, a chance to test my limits, make my mark on the world. I can't do that if I never leave the island."

"So then go, chase your dreams."

"What, just pick up and leave? Now?"

"Why not?" he challenged.

"Because...I'm not ready yet. I'm going to leave, at

some point. But right now there's school, and my job, my family—"

"Those are excuses, not reasons." She started to argue, but he held up a tanned hand, silencing her. "You could apply to school somewhere else, transfer your credits. Or take a semester off. There are jobs everywhere. And your family, assuming everyone is in good health, isn't going to wither up and die if you leave the zip code. As far as I can see, there's nothing keeping you here, assuming you really want to leave, that is."

"Of course I do." Didn't she? She wasn't making excuses; she was waiting for the right time.

"Then trust me. Just do it. Do whatever it is that makes you happy, that makes you whole."

He made it sound so easy. "Is that what you're doing?"

He was silent for a moment. Maybe she was getting too personal, too heavy, but he'd started it. Hadn't he?

"I don't know." His eyes were clouded, as if he were seeing something other than the water and mangroves around them. "In some ways I always have, if only out of self-preservation. There wasn't much point in trying to impress my parents. Even if I'd made one happy, the other would have disapproved, just on principle. And I moved too often to make any real friends, let alone worry about impressing them. I guess that was the only good thing about growing up in chaos—you learn to rely on yourself."

"And now?"

"I don't know. For a little while, I had thought maybe it was time to reach out, build some real relationships.

Maybe even settle down with someone special." He looked out over the water, his body tense. "Obviously, that didn't work out very well, and honestly, I don't think I've got it in me to try anymore."

Noah knew his words sounded cold, but there was no point in lying to her. He was done pretending, done trying to be someone he wasn't. He'd done that with Angela, and that hadn't done anyone any good. Besides, Mollie had said she was known for telling it like it is; the least he could do was return the favor. Even if it wasn't what she wanted to hear.

She seemed to consider his words as she scanned the horizon. "So you're just a lone wolf, huh?" She didn't seem upset by the idea; her shoulders were still relaxed, her limbs loose, as she steered the boat away from the main channel and into a narrower, winding section of water. Of course, why should she be? He was just one more temporary tourist to her; his views on life didn't have any importance for her.

"Yup, didn't you hear me out howling at the moon last night?"

She rolled her eyes. "I'll keep that in mind. Not sure I'm ready to break from the pack though. When I go— and I will go—I want to do it right. I don't want to have to come crawling back, tail between my legs, as it were."

"Being prepared is good," he conceded. "But there's a fine line between planning and procrastination. When I'm working on a big project, I sometimes find myself bogged down in the details, sketching out every angle when I need to just jump in and trust the details will work themselves out." He flashed her a grin. "But enough philosophy. Tell me about this place."

She'd slowed the boat while he was talking, nosing them into a quiet cove surrounded by a dense thicket of low-slung trees, their bare roots making a tangle above and below the clear water. It was like something out of a movie, exotic and yet somehow peaceful, too.

"Well, it's my favorite fishing spot. Other than that, what do you want to know?"

"For starters, what are those?" He pointed to the alien-looking trees that surrounded them. "I didn't know trees could grow in water like that, let alone salt water."

"Mangroves." She turned the engine to idle and went to the front of the boat, lifting the heavy anchor and tossing it in with a splash before he could offer to do it for her. "Red mangroves, specifically. Those freaky-looking roots keep them from drowning. Kind of like a house on stilts. And they act like a nursery for all sorts of baby fish, protecting them from bigger predators."

"And where there are fish, there are things that eat fish." As if to punctuate his words, a pair of pelicans flopped to a landing atop the nearest bunch of trees.

Mollie followed his gaze, and chuckled. "Exactly. That's why the birds hang out here, and it's why we're here. Should be enough for all of us. Grab a pole, and I'll help you get a line in the water."

"Don't think I can handle baiting my own hook?" He tried to look offended.

"Can you?"

"Um, maybe? Honestly, that was never my favorite part as a kid." He probably should be embarrassed by that but he wasn't. He didn't feel the urge to pretend or to try to fit in around Mollie. The sheer relief of just being himself in a place where no one cared who he was or wanted anything from him made the whole trip seem worthwhile. He might not be having the typical honeymoon, but he was definitely having a good time. Even if he didn't know how to put a frozen shrimp on a hook.

Mollie did, though. Sitting on the seat closest to the bait well, she took the sleek black rod with its brass fittings and braced it between her knees, a sight that was way more erotic than it should be. Then she swiftly threaded the hook through a partially thawed shrimp in a figure-eight type motion. "There you go. Now, how about a quick lesson in casting?"

"Sure." He stood and followed to the side of the boat farthest from the mangroves. "I thought you said the fish like to hide in the tree roots?"

"The little ones do, but getting your line trapped in the trees is a huge pain. Most of the time it snaps, and then a bird can get tangled in whatever is left in the branches." She patted him on the back. "Don't worry. There are plenty of fish on this side of the boat, too. Now, take the pole in your right hand, like this."

She quickly showed him how to hold the pole with one finger securing the line before releasing the wire bail that controlled the reel. He imitated her movements, finding that the muscle memory built from those trips as a kid was still there.

"Good, now just bring the tip of the pole back. No, not so stiff…that's it, you've got it!"

Without even really thinking, he released the line just as the pole swung overhead and his hook sailed out to land right in the middle of the cove. Hot damn, it was like riding a bike, you never really forgot. Thank heavens for muscle memory.

Mollie beamed, her smile as bright as the Florida sun overhead. "Great cast! You'll be a fisherman yet."

"I have to catch something first."

"You will—I have faith in you. Besides, you have an excellent teacher."

Her words proved prophetic, and what seemed like only minutes later he felt a tug on his line. The current? Or something more. A second later a harder tug gave him his answer. "I think I've got something!"

"Ooh, awesome! Keep reeling. Let's see what you got."

He had no intention of stopping; he was having too much fun. Seconds ticked by with the turning of the reel as he brought the fish closer to the boat. When it broke the water, Mollie leaned out and grabbed the line, handing him his prize, a sleek white and silver speckled fish.

"You did it! That's a spotted trout, and if it's big enough to be legal it's our dinner tonight."

He was grinning like a fool, but he didn't care. He was on a boat in Paradise, he'd caught a fish and he had a beautiful woman smiling at him. Simple pleasures, sure, but often those were the best kind.

* * *

Mollie couldn't take her eyes off of Noah. His bronze skin was shining in the bright sun, his hair ruffled by the breeze, and he was standing there like every proud fisherman before him, except he wasn't every fisherman. He was a famous artist. And yet that didn't matter, not out here. In his T-shirt and flip flops, he looked... perfect.

"So, is he big enough?"

Right, focus on the task at hand, Mollie. You're fishing, for heaven's sake; since when do you get all girly when you could be fishing?

"I'll grab the ruler, just a sec." Digging in the tackle box, she found the same folding ruler she'd used for her own first fish and measured carefully. "Fourteen inches. That's an inch under legal. Looks like he's gotta go back. Need some help unhooking him?"

"No, let me try." His brows furrowed in concentration as he carefully eased the hook back out. "Did it. See, I'm a quick learner."

"It helps that you're good with your hands." His eyes widened at the remark. "I mean, with sculpting and—oh, hell, you know what I mean. Just put the fish back in the water and pretend I didn't say that, okay?" She knew from long experience that the best way to get past one of her ill-thought-out remarks was to just acknowledge it and move on.

Smirking, he did as she instructed, proving once again he could follow instructions. If only her tongue would do the same. "Ready to try again?"

"Sure, but I'll bait it myself this time. You haven't

even gotten a line in the water yet. I can fend for myself."

"Thanks." She quickly baited her own hook and cast out into her favorite spot, watching him out of the corner of her eye. He was managing fine, which was no surprise. He really was good with his hands, which despite her protest to the contrary had her thinking about all the other ways he could use them.

Damn, she needed to cool off before she did something crazy, like make a move on him. She never did that. Guys were not interested in skinny brunettes with fish slime on their hands; they wanted blonde bombshells who got manicures and wore sundresses. Her own cutoffs were getting so frayed she'd need to throw them out soon, and her tank top was faded and plain. Her biggest nod to fashion was her extensive collection of bathing suits. It's not that she disliked shopping as much as she figured she was never going to look like a supermodel, so why bother?

Noah might make her feel good about herself, but she needed to remember she was still a small-town tomboy who probably smelled like bait. And even if he was interested, he was leaving in a week. She respected herself too much to be just an upgrade on some guy's vacation package. She needed to treat him like all the other guys she knew, a buddy, someone to have some laughs with. She could do that. She just needed to put things back in perspective.

Thankfully, when it came to perspective, she had a secret weapon. Putting her pole in one of the rod holders, she retrieved her camera bag from where she'd stowed it earlier. Her Canon Rebel was secondhand, but worked better than a lot of the newer models she'd seen tourists carrying. More importantly, she'd spent enough time with it to learn all its quirks, until it had the same familiar comfort as a favorite pair of slippers.

Noah was watching his line with the intensity of a lion stalking its prey, and she was able to snap several shots of him before he noticed.

"I wondered how long it would take you to get that thing out."

"Sorry, I don't usually sneak photos of people like that. You just looked so…." Gorgeous? Distracting? "Focused," she finished. "I can get rid of it if you want, but it's a good shot."

He shrugged. "If it's good, keep it."

It was good, she knew without looking. She'd felt that tingle that said the shot was exactly how she wanted it to be. "Thanks. And I promise I'll give you a heads-up if I aim your way again."

Glancing at her still slack line, she moved to the bow. There was an anhinga perched on a partially sinking tree stump drying its wings, just begging to be photographed. Stretching out on her belly, she steadied the camera, letting her world shrink down to the size of her viewfinder. Shot after shot, the hypnotic sound of the shutter clearing her mind. By the time the gangly bird flew off, she had a cramp in her neck and could feel the sting of a sunburn starting. No telling how long she'd been there; hopefully Noah wasn't too bored. So much for being a fun tour guide.

She rolled over and saw him reeling in his line, Baby

asleep at his feet. A minute later, he pulled up a small fish, deftly snagging it in one hand. "Are these things good to eat?"

"Oh, yeah, that's a mangrove snapper, but he's a bit too small."

"I figured, but this is the third one I've caught. The first two were bigger, but I wasn't sure what they were or if I should keep them, so I let them go. Guess I'll send this one back to his buddies." He deftly released the fish, unconcernedly watching it swim away.

"Two more? You should have said something!"

"I didn't want to break your concentration. I hate it when people interrupt me when I'm working."

She shook her head. "I appreciate that, but I'm supposed to be helping you. You could have kept those bigger ones for dinner tonight."

"I'm fine. There was nothing pressing I needed. Besides, we can still have a fish dinner."

"I don't think so." She eyed the sun, now directly overhead. "It's getting too hot to catch much now. We'd have to stay out until nearly dark if we wanted to have a chance, and I didn't bring enough food or water for that."

"You forget, there's more than one way to skin a cat. Er, fish." He winked. "Trust me. Be at the Sandpiper at six and I'll show you."

Noah stepped out of the shower and wrapped a towel around his waist. After the fishing trip this morning, he'd taken a walk on the beach, then ordered room service for lunch, staying in his room to work on some

sketches and catch up on email. He'd also used part
of the afternoon to track down the area's best seafood
restaurant. Initially he'd approached Nic, but the hotel
proprietor had deferred to his wife, explaining that Jillian had lived on the island far longer and was the better source of information.

She'd been exactly that, and he now had a reservation
for two at a place called Pete's Crab Shack and instructions to bring back a slice of key lime pie. It seemed the
mother-to-be had a craving for it. Hopefully the place
was as good as they had hyped it to be; he wanted to do
something nice for Mollie after all the time she'd spent
with him this morning.

He'd had a really good time, far better than he'd expected. She'd impressed him with her knowledge of the
plants and wildlife they'd seen, but mostly he'd just enjoyed being around her. He liked that she didn't need
him to entertain her every minute; she didn't hang on
his every word or try to flatter him. In fact, although
she probably wouldn't admit it, she'd been so relaxed
around him she'd forgotten he was there. Another guy
might be offended, but he knew what it was like to get
caught up in the moment. And having a bit of quiet time
to himself had been just fine, too.

Pulling a pair of casual but neatly pressed khakis
and a lightweight button-down shirt from the closet,
he dressed and wondered what Mollie would be wearing. So far he'd only seen her in casual clothes; would
she dress up tonight? Not that it mattered; she'd look
great in a paper bag. She didn't need to fuss with her
appearance to be a knockout; between her fine bone

structure and those Bette Davis eyes she was already there. It really was too bad she'd insisted on things staying platonic. A vacation fling with someone like her would give him memories for a lifetime.

But she had every right to draw the line, and the part of him not located below the belt respected her for doing it. She was right, he wasn't sticking around, and she deserved way better than a quick roll in the sand with the likes of him. She deserved someone with a lot less baggage and a lot more permanence.

Tonight, though, tonight she was his, if only for dinner. Grabbing his wallet, he strode out of the room, locking the door and pocketing the old-fashioned key. One more sign that the Sandpiper was sticking to its historical roots. Everything in Paradise was that way—modern enough to be functional, but with a 1950s, wholesome vibe he'd never thought to see outside of a *Leave It to Beaver* rerun. As a kid, this was the kind of place he had wanted to live. Now, it was a great place to regroup and recover.

Downstairs he avoided the cluster of travelers in the lobby, ducking out the side door instead. The humidity slapped at him as soon as he stepped onto the deck, but the temperature had dropped a bit and the forecast was for a balmy evening. Even so, the whitewashed porch offered an extra measure of comfort. The wide roof protected him from the still-warm sun and oversize paddle fans provided a constant breeze. Rambling his way past comfortable-looking patio chairs and baskets of vividly blooming orchids, he made his way to the front steps where he'd first met Mollie, just twenty-four hours ago.

And there she was, walking up the path in a pair of black jeans that looked painted on and a halter top held up by the thinnest of straps. One good tug and...well, he wasn't going to think about that. There was enough skin showing already to make him a bit weak in the knees as he descended the steps to meet her.

"I'm a little early," she apologized, "but I couldn't wait any longer—I'm starving."

"Well, then, let's get going." He kept pace with her across the parking lot, wedging himself into her tiny car. "I think I could get very used to being chauffeured around, although I'd request a bigger limo next time."

"Hey, beggars can't be choosers, and if you think I'm waiting around for a cab, you've lost your mind. I need food, stat, and you promised me a fish dinner."

"I did. We have reservations at Pete's Crab Shack. Jillian recommended it."

She glanced over at him in surprise. "I didn't think Pete's took reservations."

An uneasy feeling settled in his gut. "Is it not good? I told Jillian I wanted the best. If there's somewhere else you'd rather go, just name it."

Pulling out of the lot, she grinned. "No, Pete's is great, and it really does have the best seafood anywhere on the island. It's just not the kind of place you make reservations at." Chuckling, she patted his leg, sending heat straight to his groin. "I can't imagine what they thought when you called."

"Probably that I'm some pretentious out-of-towner who doesn't know how to blend in with the locals. Guess they're right."

"Hey, I'm flattered by the thought, even if it was un-necessary. And if we *had* needed reservations, I'd be glad you called."

"You're saying it's the thought that counts?"

"Something like that, yeah."

"Well, that's something. So, if this isn't the kind of place that takes reservations, what kind of place is it?"

She slowed and turned into a crowded parking lot. "You tell me."

Mollie parked the car and tried to see the restaurant through Noah's eyes. She hadn't lied—Pete's really did serve great food—but right about now he was probably kicking himself for his choice in venue. It sounded like he'd been expecting something fancy, and well, Pete's wasn't. Maybe she should have warned him, but she refused to be embarrassed.

The weathered wooden structure was perched pre-cariously along the dunes, looking like one good storm would tumble it right into the sea. Outdoor wooden pic-nic benches made up most of the seating, with a tiny indoor dining room that was mostly used by senior citi-zens and out-of-towners.

Noah got out of the car and scanned the building. "When Jillian told me the name, I kind of thought *shack* was a euphemism."

"Nope." She elbowed him as she walked by, head-ing for an open table in the back where they'd be able to see the ocean. "Thirty years ago, Pete started with a three-wall shack and a grill. He's changed a few things, kept up with the code requirements, but that's about it."

Sitting down, she handed him a plastic menu from the bucket sitting on the table. He took it, his eyes widening as he read the selections.

"Ginger curry mahi-mahi served over coconut rice, a snapper BLT with a citrus beurre blanc sauce, fish tacos with mango salsa—"

"Like I said, the best seafood in town." She grinned at his enthusiasm; Pete's had that effect on people. "And let that be a reminder not to judge a book by its cover."

"So noted." He set the menu down and held her gaze. "And for the record, I'm glad that we aren't at some stuffy restaurant with white linen tablecloths. I never know what fork to use."

"I don't buy it. No way you grew up with a military father and didn't learn basic table etiquette. But I'll agree that this is way better. I tend to avoid any place that expects me to wear high heels, just on principle."

"So I shouldn't expect any formal events this week?"

"Not in Paradise. You'd have to go south to Palm Beach or Miami to get that kind of scene." Was that what he'd expected on this trip? Was he bored already? "You could always get a rental car and shift your vacation there. I'm sure Nic would give you a partial refund, given the circumstances." It made sense that someone used to running in artistic circles would be bored in such a small town, but darned if she wasn't disappointed at the thought of him leaving so soon.

"Hey, who said anything about leaving?" He shifted, stretching his legs out under the table. "I'm more than comfortable right here. Unless you're trying to get rid of me?"

Relief flooded her body—and she wasn't going to analyze why. "Sorry, I guess I was getting ahead of myself, jumping to conclusions. I do that sometimes. In good news, I'm told by my friends that you get used to it." She flagged down a waitress, ready to order and restore some normalcy to the evening. "So, do you know what you want?"

He looked deliberately at her. "Everything looks good."

Wow. Heat rose on her cheeks to match the heat in his voice. Keeping her cool around him wasn't going to be easy if he kept this up. "Limit yourself to the menu, big guy."

There, see, she could handle herself. Setting her own menu aside, she waited for him to order.

"I'll have the fish tacos and one of the local beers, whichever you recommend." Turning to Mollie, he grinned ruefully. "Only one beer, I promise. You don't have to worry about getting me up the hotel steps tonight."

"Good. But I'll have an iced tea, just to be on the safe side. Designated driver and all that. And the crab cakes with a side of conch fritters, please."

"You got it. I'll be back with your drinks in a minute." The waitress left, and Mollie took a long breath, wondering what to say now. Funny how she hadn't had any problem talking to him on the boat or the beach, but tonight felt more like a date, which was stupid. All because he'd made reservations. No guy she'd eaten with had ever called to make reservations or taken her anywhere they were needed. Her contact with the male of the species had been limited to a shared pizza during a Dolphins game or a hot dog on the beach. That Noah had wanted to do something special, even if it hadn't worked out that way, had her off balance and unsure.

"So, what's next on the agenda for tomorrow?"

"Well, you choose—water or land?"

"We were on the water today, so I say land. Mix it up a bit."

"Okay, I'll pick you up at eight—the Sandpiper is on the way."

"On the way to where? What did I just agree to do? And why so early?"

Just then the waitress arrived with their drinks, and Mollie used the interruption to draw out the suspense, taking a sip of her tea as Noah eyed her warily.

"So? Out with it. Alligator wrestling? What?"

"Well, there are a few alligators..."

His eyebrows rose, and she realized she liked teasing him. Probably because he was such a good sport. "I'm friends with some people over at the Paradise Wildlife Rehab Center. I already asked, and they said I could bring you by any time for a behind-the-scenes tour."

"Rehab center, is that for sick animals or something?"

"Pretty much, yes." She watched him sip from his beer, relaxed once again. "They take in sick or injured wildlife, and volunteers help care for the animals until they are well enough to be released."

"Let me guess, you're one of the volunteers."

"Guilty as charged. I'm only there a few times a month, though. A lot of people do more. I just help with some of the permanent residents, the ones that couldn't be released. I leave the medical stuff to Jillian and Cassie."

"So college student, receptionist, photographer and now wildlife rehabilitator. Is there anything you can't do?"

The waitress returned with their food, saving Mollie from a response. Because she was beginning worry that the one thing she couldn't do was resist him.

Noah dug into the basket in front of him, his appetite heightened by the fresh, salt-tinged air of the island. One bite of the tangy, sweet tacos had his taste buds begging him to sell his apartment and move to Paradise, ASAP. He'd eaten in some fancy digs over the years, but this place was amazing. Or maybe he was just more able to appreciate it, given the company.

"So, tell me more about yourself. You said you have a sister?"

She licked a stray drop of tartar sauce off her finger, making him stiffen in his seat. "One older sister. She's a lawyer like our dad. Very by the book, always got perfect grades, had a scholarship to college, that kind of thing."

"And your parents expected you to do the same?" he guessed.

"At first they did. I think they're finally starting to realize that just isn't me. At least I hope so, 'cause it's never going to happen."

She offered him what he assumed was a conch fritter, and he accepted, biting into the spicy fried confection while she talked.

"But you can see how my—what was it they called it…unconventionalism?—would be unsettling compared to all that."

"Sounds like I might have gotten off easy as an only child. I always wanted a sibling, but I think you've convinced me otherwise."

She bit her lip, a habit that was quickly driving him insane.

"It isn't all bad. Dani can't help being who she is, and she always stuck up for me when we were growing up. She's just naturally driven."

"Right, and you're just a total slacker, what with school and your job and volunteering—"

"None of which have long-term potential, according to the most recent lecture from my father. But really, it's okay. They just worry."

Maybe so, but they didn't sound very supportive. "Still, it has to be hard, knowing you aren't living up to their expectations. Even if their expectations are all wrong for you. I know my military father sure as hell didn't expect his son to become an artist, that's for sure."

Mollie's eyes sparked in indignation. "Doesn't he know how amazing your work is? How amazing you are?"

She was sexy when she was pissed, all hot and bothered on his behalf. She'd be fiery like that in bed, too, no doubt about it. Too bad that idea had been tabled. Draining his beer, he reminded himself that it was his crappy relationship skills that had gotten him into this situation in the first place; he didn't need things to go from bad to worse by scaring off the first person to make him laugh in a long time. "I appreciate the compliment, but my father, like yours, has his own definition of success. But forget about them. How about we order some dessert and take it back to the inn? I'm under orders to bring back some key lime pie for Jillian. Might as well pack up something for everyone."

"Distracting me with dessert?"

"Maybe. Is it working?" He'd certainly rather discuss that than his family life.

"Is there a woman it wouldn't work on?"

"A woman on a diet?"

"Lucky for me, I tend towards bony, not plump, because their key lime pie really is the best. We should get a whole pie or maybe two, given how strong Jillian's cravings can be. That way, you and I can share one, and Nic can fight Jillian for part of hers."

Her hearty appetite was just one more thing he liked about her. And no matter what she said, she wasn't bony. Just slender, with a hint of curves that seduced the eye rather than shouting their presence. A level of nuance that appealed to the man and the artist.

It was driving him crazy not to touch her, but he'd promised to keep his hands to himself, and he was a man of his word. The question was, could he handle being around her like this, day after day, without driving himself crazy in the process? A week was starting to seem like a very long time.

Frustrated, he ordered two key lime pies and paid the

bill, insisting meals were included in her nonexistent tour-guide salary. That had gotten another laugh out of her, a laugh that he was finding as addicting as everything else about her. On the drive home, she pointed out more of natural beauty of the island, but the only beauty he was interested in was sitting right there in the driver's seat. Being this close, he could smell the coconut and vanilla scent he already associated with her; hell, he could practically taste her. And he wanted to taste her.

By the time they arrived at the hotel, he knew he wasn't going to be able to keep this up, not with the rules she'd set in place. Maybe that made him weak, but she was too potent a drug for him resist. Jaw clamped tight, he walked with her up the steps of the inn, carrying the pies and listening to her chatter about their plans for tomorrow. Plans he was going to have to break. Maybe he would rent a car, drive somewhere else, out of reach of temptation. Or maybe he'd just take an earlier flight home, and forget the whole idea of a solo honeymoon.

"Noah, did you hear me?" Mollie had stopped in front of the carved wooden doors and was staring at him, face turned up to the moonlight and looking like the fairy sprite he'd imagined her to be at their first meeting. Something not quite real, and definitely not of the same world as him.

"I'm sorry, I was just... Can we sit down?" He gestured to a love seat tucked into a corner of the porch between two potted palms.

"Um, sure." She looked down at the pies he was holding. "Should we take these in first?"

"No, just let me do this, please." He needed to say this while his brain was still in control of his libido. Sitting on the edge of the cushion, he looked out over the railing, knowing that if he faced her he'd never be able to stick to his good intentions. "I don't think we should go to the rehab center tomorrow."

Mollie shrugged beside him. "That's fine. We can do something else. Kite boarding, maybe? Or snorkeling? What did you have in mind?"

"No, I mean we shouldn't do anything together. It was really nice of you to offer to be my tour guide, but I don't think it's a good idea to continue." He took a step back towards the stairs; he needed to leave before this got even more awkward.

"What?" Mollie jumped up to stand in front of him, her arms out as if she could physically block him in. He'd have laughed if he wasn't feeling so sick about the whole thing. "What made you change your mind? Because I thought we were having a good time here." Her tone was angry, but he could see the hurt in her eyes. "Was I wrong about that?"

"Damn it, no, you weren't wrong. That's the problem."

She cocked her head, looking at him like he'd grown a second head. "Let me get this straight. You want to cancel our agreement because you're having too good a time? Are you feeling guilty because you were supposed to be here with your ex? Because there's nothing wrong with enjoying yourself, having a little fun."

"No, it's not about guilt." He ran a hand through his hair, trying to figure out how to explain things without sounding like a hormone-crazed teenager. "It's a bit more basic than that. The bald truth is…I'm attracted to you."

She grinned, her shoulders relaxing. "Okay, well, I think you're attractive, too. I mean, we had that great kiss and all. Obviously there is some chemistry. But I thought we decided that was a bad idea, that we'd just ignore that and have fun as friends."

"We did. I promised to keep things platonic, and I intend to stick to that promise. Which is why I can't see you anymore." He paused, needing her to understand. "Sweetheart, I'm at the point where ignoring it isn't an option anymore. So I'm backing out now, before I do something I regret."

"Something you regret?" she parroted his words back to him slowly, as if trying them on for size. "Like what?"

Fisting his hands in his pockets, it took every last bit of his control to keep from showing her exactly what he meant. "Like kissing you silly, right here in the moonlight, where anyone could see."

She froze, her pupils dilating at his words. "Which we agreed was a mistake. Neither of us is looking for a relationship, and you're leaving soon anyway."

He nodded. Even if he did feel like a creep, it was better to be honest.

"So, now I'm supposed to thank you for your honesty and let you leave."

"Something like that."

She bit her lip, worrying at it, and he had to clench his jaw to keep from groaning at the sight. "Then we have a problem, because I've never been very good at doing what I'm supposed to do."

Mollie meant to give Noah time to digest what she'd said, to let him respond. But he looked way too good, and the night was only so long. So she took matters into her own hands and climbed up onto his lap, straddling him on the floral couch.

"What do you think you're doing?" He wasn't moving, but she could feel the tension vibrating through him, feel how much he wanted this.

"I'm making a mistake," she whispered, lowering herself closer to his mouth. "A really good mistake."

At the first touch of lips, she felt the dam inside him burst, and all the energy he'd had vibrating below the surface was suddenly focused directly on her. His mouth fed on hers like he was a starving man and she was the last morsel of food on earth. He tasted and teased with his tongue, and all she could think was *more*. She needed more.

Her hands wove through his hair as she settled farther onto his lap, pressing herself against him as they kissed. He gripped her hips and held her in place, pinning their bodies together. Her eyes closed, Mollie ran her hands down his chest, needing to touch more of him.

Sensing her need, he leaned back to give her more access. Now she could work her hands under his shirt, skimming the muscles honed by hard work and heavy welding tools. She wasn't a virgin; she'd had her share of fumblings on the beach with boys that were more curious than passionate. But Noah was no boy; he was all hard, hot man. And he wanted her just as much as she wanted him. He didn't see her as a problem to be fixed or an issue to be dealt with. He saw her as a woman, and that alone was enough to have her ready to take him upstairs.

He was thinking along the same lines if his hands kneading her ass were any indication. Pulling away from his mouth, she worked tiny kisses up his jaw, nipping the delicate skin just below his ear. "We should go to your room," she whispered as he moved one big hand under her shirt.

"What?" he muttered, his fingers working the clasp of her bra.

"Your room. We should go there before Jillian or Nic finds us naked on the patio."

Her words finally seemed to penetrate, and he stilled, breathing hard. A moment later, he lifted her off of him onto the other side of the couch.

"Noah? Are you okay?"

"Yes… No. I'm sorry. I can't take you up to my room."

"What?" She hadn't imagined that kiss—he wanted her, she knew he did. She'd felt it, felt him. "Are you worried about Jillian or Nic? Trust me, they don't care. And the rooms are soundproof."

At that comment he froze, and she saw his eyes go dark. But then he shook his head and stood, turning his back to her as he leaned on the railing, catching his breath.

Straightening her shirt, Mollie walked over to stand alongside him. "Hey, you're going to have to make up your mind here. First, you say you're too attracted to be friends, then we're kissing like the world's going to end, then you're pushing me away." She bumped him with her shoulder. "You're kind of giving mixed signals here, but if you're expecting me to apologize for that kiss, I'm not going to."

He grinned, his features softening with the movement. "You'd better not. That was possibly the best kiss of my life."

"Just possibly? Should we try again to make sure?" This was totally out of her norm, but hey, go big or go home. She was up for another try as long as he wasn't going to flash hot and cold again.

Gripping the balcony, he sighed. "I'm sorry. I know I'm not making much sense here. But believe me. I want you in every single way."

Her toes curled at the intensity of his voice. "But?"

"But like you said before, casual sex isn't a good idea. I learned that lesson the hard way. Not that you're anything like Angela," he hastened to correct, "but sex can have consequences. Consequences that neither of us is in a place to deal with right now."

He really looked at her then, and she saw the determination in his eyes as well as the longing. She sighed. He was right. Damn it. She hated when common sense kept her from having fun. "Then where does that leave us?" Her stomach clenched; she wasn't sure what answer she wanted to hear, but she knew he'd be honest with her. He'd proven that to her.

"Well," he drawled, trailing a finger from her cheek down to her lips. "There's just friends, and there's making love, and there's all whole lot of space in between.

Maybe we can play it by ear, and find our way down the middle?"

She shivered, fighting the urge to lean into him. She needed to get this straight. She was in uncharted waters and didn't want to run aground on some hidden reef. "So you're saying we'd be...what? Dating? And then what?"

He sobered. "And then I leave. But I've got until the end of the week, and I'd like to spend it with you. And I don't want to be fighting the urge to kiss you the whole time."

So, this was it. She could take what he was offering for now, and then he'd be gone. Or she could say goodbye to him now, and never see him again. Put that way, it really wasn't even a choice. "So are you going to kiss me again, or what?"

Noah did kiss her, thoroughly and with great pleasure. Having Mollie in his arms, with the stars above and sound of the waves crashing in the background, was definitely a high point of his vacation. Hell, a high point of his life. But at some point a light had turned on inside and Mollie had insisted they needed to take Jillian her pie. He had offered to buy the woman a dozen of them tomorrow if they could stay outside making out, but Mollie had just laughed and dragged him inside.

So now he was eating pie at the big wooden table in the Sandpiper kitchen with way too many people. Well, just Jillian and Nic, but that was two too many, as far as he was concerned.

"This is exactly what the baby wanted. Thank you,

Noah." Jillian scraped the last bite off of her plate and reached for another slice. "But I'm holding you responsible when you have to roll me out of here at nine months. I have zero self-control when it comes to sweets right now."

"Eat what you want," Nic responded, placing a glass of milk in front of her. "You barely picked at dinner and didn't have much more at lunch. Besides," he said with a wink, "I like you a little plump."

Jillian smacked his shoulder, but her laugh tempered the rebuke. In truth she looked beautiful, and everyone in the room knew it.

"Please, at least you have an excuse." Mollie dug a fork into the pie that she and he were sharing, forgoing cutting a slice to eat directly from the pan. "I'm only eating for one and I'm pretty sure I've outpaced you."

Her innocent comment had him wondering what she would look like, heavy with child. He pushed the ridiculous thought away, but not before longing hit him solidly in the gut. But this time it wasn't for the marriage and family he'd lost. This was a new fantasy, one that centered on the slip of a woman sitting beside him. He gulped from a glass of ice water, suddenly realizing that sex wasn't the only way to complicate things. Feelings did that, too.

Needing to change the subject, Noah looked to Nic across the table. "So, I hear you were born into the hotel industry, more or less."

"That's right. My father made hotels his business before I was born. When I got out of college, I joined him, working my way up the ladder. But by the time I came to Paradise I was ready for a change."

Noah tipped his head. "Doesn't seem like you got too far away from the family business. You stayed in hotels, just on a smaller scale."

Nic grinned. "I figured it made sense to play to my strengths. But the big change is that now I'm in one place, setting down roots. Before, I lived out of my suitcase more than my apartment. Every time I got a new hotel just how I wanted it, I'd have to leave and move on to the next one. Now, when I fix something, make it better, I get to stick around and enjoy it."

"Is that what made you quit and buy this place? You wanted to settle down?" He ate another bite of pie, following Mollie's example and taking right from the tin.

"Basically. Buying the Sandpiper was my wedding gift to Jillian."

"Caruso Hotels was going to tear it down," Jillian broke in. "Nic knew how important this place was to me, so he bought it himself instead."

"And I'm going to be paying the bank for it for quite some time," he replied shaking his head ruefully, but gripping his wife's hand where it lay on the table. The love between them was obvious, the kind of love that overcame whatever obstacles it encountered.

"It was a wonderful thing to do, and I'll never forget it." Jillian fanned her eyes in a vain attempt to stem the tears that were spilling onto her cheeks. "I'm sorry, it's the hormones. I cry over everything now."

Mollie got up and got Jillian a tissue from the box on the counter. "Hey, no crying. It all worked out okay. The Sandpiper is still here, better than ever. And now you've got your own home being built, and it's all going to be picture-perfect. You and Cassie have everything so wrapped up I may have to run off and join the circus just to even things out."

Jillian giggled, her tears forgotten, and he had a sneaking suspicion that had been Mollie's goal. "You will not. You're going to find your own guy and settle down, too. And I'm going to say 'I told you so' when it happens."

Mollie made a gagging noise, causing every to join in on the laughter. But Noah wondered how much of what she said was for comedy's sake. She'd said before she wanted adventure. Well, he knew a bit about that. He'd been known to pick up and move just because he'd gotten tired of the color of his apartment walls, and unlike Nic, he'd enjoyed the constant variety. Maybe he and Mollie didn't have to end things when she left; maybe they could have some adventures together. She could come see him in Atlanta, or he could close up the studio for a while and take her on an extended trip somewhere, show her some of his favorite places. He wasn't quite ready to go there yet, but it was something to keep in mind.

Jillian stood, a hand pressed to her lower back as she angled her way upright. "You two are welcome to keep chatting, but it's past my bedtime." She started for the private section of the inn. "Oh, and Mollie, could you give me a hand for a second? I need your opinion on the curtains for the nursery."

Mollie followed Jillian down the hall, far enough to be out of earshot of the men. "All right, we both know I have zero opinions when it comes to curtains, so what's up?"

"That wasn't very believable, huh?"

"Not at all. But seriously, is everything okay? You're scaring me." Was there something wrong with the baby, something she did want to make public?

"I'm fine." Jillian smoothed down the front of her maternity shirt, a small smile lifting her lips as she rubbed her rounded belly. "It's you I'm worried about."

"Me?"

"Yes, you. The chemistry between you and Noah was so thick I could have served it with the pie. What's going on with you guys?"

What *was* going on with them? "It's…complicated. But it's fine. I've got it under control. Just a little summer fling with a hot guy. After all, not all of us are ready to get married and have our two point five children."

Jillian blanched, tears threatening to return.

Crap. "Oh, Jillian, I'm sorry! I didn't mean it that way. I'm happy for you, I really am. And for Cassie. But I'm in a different place, and I'd like you to be happy for me, too." Wanting to kick herself for making her friend cry, she gave her a hug. "Everything is going to be fine, I promise."

Jillian nodded and gestured towards the kitchen. "Well, then, go get him. And make sure you tell me every detail once this fling of yours is over. As an old, matronly lady, I need to live vicariously through you."

"It's a deal. We'll have a girls' night after he leaves— you, me and Cassie. I promise." Impulsively, she gave her one last squeeze, then hurried back to find Noah and Nic bonding over some single-malt scotch, telling stories about their travels. Nic didn't have a lot of guy friends in the area yet; it was nice to see him finding someone to talk to.

"Hey, boys, I'm off." Standing on her toes she reached up to give Noah a goodnight kiss. The open display of affection had Nic choking on his whiskey— apparently he wasn't as insightful as his wife and hadn't picked up on the aforementioned chemistry. "Don't keep him up too late, Nic. I'm picking Noah up at eight, and if he's hungover, I'll know who to blame."

She needn't have worried. Noah was standing on the steps waiting for her when she pulled up the next morning, looking rested and ready to work in a pair of jeans and a surf shirt she suspected he'd purchased just for this trip. Better yet, he had a cup of coffee in each hand. A sexy man bearing caffeine—did it get any better than that?

Idling in front of the inn, she accepted the travel mug he handed her as he got in. The bold flavor rolled over her tongue, waking her much more thoroughly than her alarm clock and a five-minute shower had. By the time they reached the turn-off to the rehab center, she was fully caffeinated and ready to go.

Her small car bumped over the hills and ruts in the gravel road, banging Noah's knees against the dash. "You've have got to get a bigger car. If not for my sake, then for Baby's."

"Baby's fine. He likes my car." She darted a glance to the rearview mirror and checked that the big doofus really was fine. He had his head poked forward, trying to catch the breeze from Noah's open window, drooling all over the rear seat. She'd have to hit the car wash again. And look into protective seat covers—waterproof ones.

"He'd like a big SUV better," Noah mumbled, rubbing his battered leg as best he could, given the close confines. "Thank goodness everywhere on Paradise Isle is a short drive."

She rolled her eyes at him and parked in the small, shaded lot. Directly in front of them was the main hospital and office building, their first destination of the morning. "Okay, everyone out. We'll leave Baby in the office. They love him here, but he has a tendency to spook the animals."

"Shocking."

She elbowed him. "I told you before, it's not his fault he's big. But you're right, he is a bit intimidating. Luckily the office staff knows he's nothing but a big teddy bear."

Mollie led the way into the simple wooden building, pointing out a small, tasteful plaque with the Sandpiper Inn logo near the door. "They had to put on a new roof a few months ago, and the Sandpiper donated most of the materials. Nic actually came out and helped with the installation, as well. Some of the animal enclosures are sponsored by other local businesses."

There weren't many people in the office at this hour, or really any hour. It was a bare-bones kind of operation. But Tara, an intern from the University of Florida, and Dylan, the director, were already hard at work, bent over a spreadsheet that, she was willing to guess showed too little money coming in and too much going out. It was always that way, but somehow Dylan managed to make it work. He had an MBA from Harvard and a magic touch when it came to soliciting donations. His charm and good looks didn't hurt, of course. Once upon a time, she'd had a crush on him, but he'd never seen her as anything but a friend. Now, looking at the bleach-blond hair spilling over his blue eyes, she didn't feel anything. No, it was the dark, brooding artist beside her that had her heart racing and her girly parts keeping time.

Baby, however, still had a thing for the guy, and was currently trying to squirm his considerable girth in between Dylan and his cheap metal desk. The scrape of aluminum on terrazzo flooring made it clear Baby wasn't taking no for an answer.

"Baby, stop that! Have a little dignity, for heaven's sake."

Ignoring her, the big pooch flopped down in the space he'd created, rolling over to beg a belly rub. Unfazed, Dylan, who'd known Baby almost as long as Mollie had, just leaned down and scratched the dog while continuing to pore over the numbers in front of him. "Hi, Dylan, sorry to interrupt." She gave a pointed look at Baby. "But I wanted to see if there was anything you need me to do while I'm here."

He looked up from his desk, as if finally noticing her. "Hey, I didn't think you were on the schedule today."

"I'm not. But I'm giving Noah here a tour, and figured I might as lend a hand if you needed it."

"That's right. You did say you might bring someone by. Sorry, it's been a bit crazy here. Not that that's any different than usual." He stood, extending a tanned hand to Noah. "Nice to meet you."

Mollie watched the two men shake hands and nearly sighed. They were both beautiful specimens of the male gender, one blond, one dark, both simmering with testosterone and some undeniable quality that made men so interesting. But only one of them made her toes tingle when he looked at her. Which, given the circumstances, was one too many. Still, she couldn't help but hope that he'd see some of what she saw in this place, that he'd get why she came here week after week. Too often, she was the odd one out, the misfit, but here the animals accepted her for who she was. No one else in her life did that.

Except for Noah.

Damn, she was in serious trouble.

Noah shook the proffered hand, then looked around the room. The floors were bare, and the office furniture the staff used was thrift-store chic at best, but there were some hand-carved chairs for visitors and an amazing array of framed wildlife photos lining the walls, each with a name plaque beneath it. "Mollie says you do some good work here."

The taller man shook his head. "Not me—I just try to keep the roof from caving in, sometimes literally. Our volunteers do all the real work. Like Mollie, she's our official, but unpaid, photographer. The framed prints and postcards she lets us sell raise quite a bit of money, and she took all the photos on the website, too."

So she was the one behind the gorgeous pictures

hanging on the walls. Still listening, he moved in to get a closer look, a germ of an idea forming in his head.

"She also developed an operational conditioning program that's she's teaching to all the other volunteers. We're incredibly lucky to have someone of her skill here."

Mollie blushed. "I do some clicker training with the animals and taught the other staff how. It's not rocket science."

"What's clicker training?"

"It's a form of operant conditioning," Dylan explained. "It uses positive reinforcement to get the animal to offer the behavior you're looking for without stressing them out. Lots of trainers do it, with domestic and zoo animals, but some are better than others. Mollie's one of the best. Speaking of which…" He grabbed a sticky note off his desk. "Since you're here, could you swing by Simba's enclosure? He's refusing to go into the holding area, and Krissy can't get in there to clean. I was going to try to make it down there myself in a bit…"

"But you've got your hands full. No problem, I'm on it." She swiped a lanyard off a peg in the wall and waved goodbye to Tara. Dylan was already back at work and didn't seem to notice them leaving. Noah would be offended, but he wasn't exactly a people-pleaser himself when he was working. He understood intensity first hand. As did Mollie, who was already halfway out of the room, intent on helping Simba, whoever that was.

Following her to the back door of the office, he was amused to see that Baby had positioned himself directly under Dylan's desk and was now operating as a living footrest. The big beast was so docile he was practically inert.

The rest of the building seemed to be a combination of an animal hospital and wildlife cafeteria. Chrome cages, several holding injured wildlife, lined the walls. He spotted a pelican with a bandaged wing, a turtle with a cracked shell held together with what looked like modeling clay, and a very small squirrel. Other cages had towels draped across their fronts, perhaps to shade the more nocturnal species from the bright fluorescent lighting. The back wall, where Mollie had headed, held a long chrome counter top and a large sink. Under the counter were several small refrigerators as well as storage cabinets he assumed held dry goods or other equipment. A teenage boy with red hair and freckles was busy chopping up vegetables, while another boy, shorter and rounder, weighed out the food and placed it in metal dishes.

"Hey, Andy, Tom, how's it going?" Mollie greeted the boys, then dug into one of the refrigerators, pulling out a baggie of what looked like chopped meat.

"Hi, Mollie," the stockier boy replied, a big grin on his face. His friend just nodded, his face blushing nearly as red as his hair. He wondered if Mollie knew they had the hots for her and realized immediately she'd never show it if she did. She wouldn't want to embarrass them like that. "I heard Simba's giving Krissy a hard time again. You going to help her?"

Mollie held up the baggie. "I'm going to try. If not, we'll just leave that cage for tomorrow. No one goes in there, okay?" She waited until both boys had nodded their understanding before leading him out the back door onto a mulch covered path.

"So, what's a Simba?" Images from *The Lion King* flashed in his head as they passed by wooden and steel habitats housing an assortment of wildlife.

"Simba is a very beautiful, very traumatized Florida panther. He was being held as a pet illegally until Fish and Wildlife got a tip from a neighbor." Her stride quickened in visible agitation. "The man who owned him had starved him and used a Taser on him. He was terrified of people when he came here, and sometimes he still gets panicked." She stopped at a large, fenced-in area, anger and pain radiating off of her. "I don't understand how anyone can be that cruel."

He kept his silence; as far as he was concerned, jail was too good for someone that abused animals. But saying that wasn't going to help, so he just squeezed her hand in sympathy.

Beyond the fence a shadow moved, and he caught his breath. There, only a few yards away, a big tawny cat paced from one end of his territory to the other, eyes darting as if looking for danger. That such a large, powerful predator could be so anxious was just wrong; he could see why Mollie was so angry. It was disgusting the way some people treated animals.

Mollie wasn't showing her anger now, though. She'd turned it off somehow, exuding a calm confidence as she climbed over the low railing along the path and worked her way right up to the fence.

Oh hell, she wasn't going in there with the panther—was she? He'd learned to trust her judgment over the past few days, but every protective instinct in his body was screaming for him to stop her. But if he said something, she'd know he doubted her, and that would make him as bad as all the other people who had tried to control her life. He couldn't—he wouldn't—do that. Fisting his hands in his pockets to keep from grabbing her back to safety, he waited and prayed he'd made the right choice.

Chapter Two

Mollie could sense Noah's tension as she approached the big cat, but she couldn't stop to reassure him right now. All her focus was on Simba and on convincing him she wasn't a threat. She'd been working with him off and on for months, and although he'd filled out and healed physically, mentally he still had scars. Which meant she would *not* be going in the enclosure with him. Simba's training was done via protected contact—panther on one side of the fence, her on the other.

"Hey, big boy. What's wrong, having a bad day?" She kept her voice low, her movements slow and measured. When she finally reached the fence, she slid down into a sitting position and watched him, hoping he'd stop his pacing long enough to recognize her as the friend she was. At first, he ignored her, his eyes clouded with past pain. But she kept up a steady stream of chatter, telling him about Noah, about her job, anything she could think of. It was the tone that mattered, not the words. At this point she wasn't training, just connecting. A brain can't learn when it's overwhelmed by stress or fear, so she needed to wait for a signal that he'd downgraded from anxious to cautious.

Finally, the big cat stopped his patrolling and truly looked at her, one ear twitching in recognition. This was it; he was ready to work. Reaching into the baggie she'd set beside her, she threaded a piece of meat onto the end of a long stick. "Kebabs, panther style," she whispered to Noah. His stifled chuckle had her watching Simba for a reaction, but the cat was now more concerned with the meat than stranger danger.

His whiskers twitching, Simba scented the air.

"That's it, big guy, you know the drill. Come to Mama."

A few seconds passed without movement. Maybe he wasn't going to do it today. She could try again tomorrow, but damn it, she didn't want to give up. Not yet.

Then, as if moving in slow motion, he took a single cautious step towards her.

Click! She used the noisemaker around her neck to mark the behavior and threaded the meat-on-a-stick through the holes in the fence as far as she could. Simba had to move even closer to reach it, so she clicked again and gave him another reward. The familiar game seemed to ease the old anxieties, and within minutes he was close enough for her to feel his warm breath on her face.

She heard Noah stand up, and waved him back. "It's fine," she reassured him, using much the same tone as she had with the panther. "The fence will hold." Besides, Simba wasn't looking to cause any trouble now. He was smart, and now that he'd settled down was more than happy to work for his food.

She took out the collapsible targeting stick she carried in her pocket, extending it the full eighteen inches of length. A rubber ball on the end acted as a focus point, and the second she offered it to him he turned and touched it with his nose. Another click, another chunk of meat. "Good boy. Now let's make it a little harder." She slowly stood up, discreetly stretching out the kinks before offering the target again, this time several feet higher. Without missing a beat, the big cat put his massive paws up on the fence to reach it. Click and reward.

Moving several steps to the right, she repeated the targeting game a few more times. Only when the cat was eagerly moving wherever she directed him did she move towards the holding area built against the back of the enclosure. This was where the keepers put the animals when they needed to clean or otherwise work in the larger part of the habitat. It kept the animals out of trouble and the keepers safe—if you could get the animal in there. Which was why Mollie had worked with all the volunteers to teach them the targeting routine she was putting Simba through now. Most of the staff and animals had picked it up pretty quickly, but some, like Simba, took a little more time and patience.

Krissy was pretty new and had probably rushed this morning, not recognizing Simba's agitation. Luckily, now he was cooperating, and she was able to take baby steps, clicking and rewarding the whole way, right up to the entrance of the holding pen. This was the real test. After being kept in a small cage for so long by his former owner, he preferred the open. But his enclosure needed to be cleaned and restocked for his own good.

She held her breath and moved to the gate of the smaller structure, the target held where Simba would have to enter the pen in order reach it. Biting her lip, her hand shook slightly, making the red ball waver. Simba paused, and she silently urged him on, cheering for him in her head. Then, as if it had been his own idea all along, he padded in and touched the target, letting Mollie close the gate behind him before accepting the rest of the meat as his reward.

"You did it!" She pumped her fist, wishing she could hug the silly beast.

"He did. And you did—that was amazing." Noah was grinning ear to ear, and without thinking she wrapped her arms around him, giving him the celebratory hug she wished she could give Simba.

Noah hugged Mollie, letting his initial concern and admiration heat into something more primal. There was no way he could have that tight body pressed against him without reacting. She felt his response and looked up, surprise flashing in her eyes before she pulled his head down for the kiss they both wanted. He let her take control, holding himself back as she explored his mouth, fisting his hands in her shirt to keep them still.

His heart was pounding hard in his ears when she finally lifted her head and smiled at him.

"So, what do you think?"

"I think that we should do that more often," he teased.

She gave him a half-hearted push. "No, about Simba. Isn't he gorgeous?"

"I don't know, I think you've got him beat, looks-wise. But he is impressive. You about gave me a heart attack when you walked up to the fence like that."

"Sorry." She shrugged. "I should have warned you what to expect. But trust me, I'm not going to put myself in any danger."

"Good." His shoulders relaxed a bit.

"If Simba hurt me, who knows what would happen to him? I couldn't take that chance."

"Wait, you didn't go in there because you were afraid for him, not yourself?" Her logic was giving him an ulcer. "He could kill you with one swipe of his claws."

She tensed, her eyes narrowing at him. "He's not a bad animal, and it's not his fault what happened to him. This is his chance at a better life, and I'm not going to do anything to screw it up."

Noah shook his head. "Fine. Whatever your reasons, I'm just glad you're going to be safe. I don't want to turn on the evening news one day and find out you got eaten by an alligator or something."

"I promise," she swore, tracing a cross on her chest with her finger. "Now, time for the real work. It shouldn't take me too long to clean out his enclosure—

you're welcome to take a walk and check out the other animals. I can come find you when I'm done."

She thought he was going to go play tourist while she sweated and did manual labor? He hadn't planned on scooping panther poop on his vacation, but he also wasn't going to sit by and let a women half his size do all the heavy lifting. "I'll help. Just show me what to do."

Forty-five minutes later, he'd scooped, scraped and hosed down the enclosure. Mollie, in turn, had scrubbed out the giant water bowl, fetched Simba's meal and vitamins from the main building, and placed what she called enrichment objects, basically industrial-sized cat toys as far as he could tell, all around the enclosure. She'd even scrambled up a tree to hang a rope from a low branch. The last step had involved them hiding the cat's food all around the enclosure—inside hollow logs, under piles of branches and even hanging from what looked like an oversize clothespin on the rope she'd put up. He was hot, sweaty, and probably smelled like panther poop and raw meat, but the look of satisfaction on Mollie's face made it all worth it.

"Done. Now we just have to let him back in."

"As long as we're getting out first, that's fine." He led the way back out, carrying the cleaning supplies and empty food bucket while she made sure the lock was secure, then watched her slide back the gate that had kept the oversize cat contained.

Wasting no time, Simba loped back out, but instead of pacing this time he circled more methodically, sniffing around until he discovered one of the hidden food caches. "He looks happy."

Mollie smiled, rocking back on her heels as she watched. "He does, doesn't he? Thank you for letting me take the time to do this and for helping with all the cleaning. You didn't have to do that."

"I know, but I wanted to." She'd put a spell on him, just as she'd done with the wild animal in there. Like the panther, he'd been hurt and licking his wounds when he met her, his head full of anger and betrayal. But she'd seen past that and had accepted him right where he was. From the start, her easy manner and natural confidence had seeped under his skin, winning him over before he'd even thought to protect himself. Her boss had said she was the best, and given how quickly she'd wrapped him around her little finger, he believed it.

Something about her just eased the ragged edges deep inside, soothing him when he hadn't realized he needed soothing. Like the panther, he'd come to Paradise wary, but none of that had mattered once he looked into Mollie's eyes.

He was in trouble, no way around it. Wanting something this badly meant being vulnerable, meant hurting. He'd learned never to hold on too tight, to wish too hard—too many moves and too many broken promises littered his past to believe otherwise. But today, standing in the sunshine with a sprite of a woman, surrounded by wounded and healed animals, it was a little too easy to believe in second chances and happily-ever-afters.

"Everything okay?" She squinted up at him, her innocence and beauty nearly knocking him out. "I was thinking we'd get this stuff put away, wash up, and then I'd give you that tour. No more mucking out cages, I promise."

He'd shovel crap all day, if that's what she wanted to do. "I'd like that. But then I'm taking you to lunch. Maybe kebabs... I'm having an odd craving for them all of a sudden."

He got the laugh he was going for and spent the rest of the morning being introduced to an incredible assortment of native Florida wildlife. The alligators he'd expected, as well as a variety of other animals—opossums, armadillos, bobcats, raccoons, pelicans and even a bald eagle that was missing part of a wing. All looked happy, despite being either too injured or too traumatized to survive on their own. Just like Baby, who had handled the transition to three legs better than some people handled a broken fingernail. He knew that part of the ability to push on, heal and survive was due to their innate resilience.

But he was beginning to think that it was more than that. They couldn't have recovered without the help of people like Mollie, without a support system. Relying on others hadn't made them weak; it had given them strength. He'd spent a lifetime keeping people at a distance in an attempt to protect himself. Hell, he'd even kept his fiancée at arm's length.

Of course, just because he was ready to let down his guard and start reaching didn't mean Mollie felt the same way. She'd told him from the beginning she was looking to spread her wings, not get tied down.

If he wanted any kind of chance at all, he needed to back off and let her take the lead.

Mollie was relieved to see that Baby hadn't caused any problems in the office since they left him. Not that he was a bad dog—she'd worked hard on his training— but his size alone could lead to issues in small, enclosed spaces. He had a habit of knocking things over with his tail, which was tabletop height, not to mention his tendency to move furniture just by leaning on it. But today he'd just napped, opening one eye lazily when she called his name, then insisting on giving a slobbery goodbye to everyone in the room before following her and Noah back to the car.

She loaded him up, then blasted the AC in a vain attempt to cool off. Noah looked just as sweaty, but in that sexy way that only worked on men. Women just got gross. Not the look she was going for. "Minor problem. I know you said you wanted to go to lunch, but we can't take Baby inside a restaurant, and it's too hot to sit outside. Maybe I should just drop you off at the inn? Or we could go drop Baby off, and then find somewhere to eat."

Noah's stomach growled in response. "I'm too hungry to wait that long. Why don't we pick up something to go, then take it back to the inn? Assuming Baby can come in there, of course."

"He can. It's practically his second home. And he loves to play with Murphy. But are you sure you're okay with takeout?"

"I'm sure. Let's just go get it before I die of starvation, okay?"

"Okay."

In the end, Mollie ran into a local deli while Noah stayed in the air-conditioned car with the dog. Five minutes later and they were back at the inn, Baby nearly tripping over his own feet in his mad dash up the stairs.

"Do you want to eat in the kitchen or on the porch? It's cooler inside, but we might have more privacy out here."

Noah headed for the front door, carrying the bags from the deli. "Cool sounds good right now, and I don't mind sharing. Besides, Baby is dying to get inside."

The mastiff was sitting in front of the door, whimpering in a very unmasculine way.

"Move over, and I'll open the door." She gently nudged the dog out of the way with her foot and opened the front door, leading Noah through the main lobby into the kitchen, Baby impatiently bringing up the rear.

A loud woof sounded from the back of the inn, and then a blur of black and white fur whizzed into the room. Ecstatic, Baby returned the greeting, then set to sniffing every inch of the smaller dog.

Noah found a rope toy and tried to instigate a three-way game of tug while Mollie spread out the food on the counter. "We've got smoked fish dip and crackers, club sandwiches, pasta salad, fruit, and rolls. Oh, and some cookies for dessert."

"Sounds good, I'll have some of everything." Leaving the dogs to play, he washed up and joined her at the counter, heaping a plate with, as he'd said, everything. He reached across her for a second cookie, his arm brushing her chest just enough to shift her appetite from food to him. Oblivious, he shoved the cookie in his mouth, leaning one hip against the counter.

"Dessert first?"

"Is that a problem?" he asked, one crumb sticking to corner of his mouth.

"Nope." She stood on her tiptoes and licked it off, watching his eyes go cloudy with desire. "Life is short. You have to enjoy it while you can."

He growled in agreement, then lifted her onto the counter, trapping her with his body. Her legs wrapped around his waist as he feasted on her mouth. Chocolate and sin, that's what he tasted like. She let herself get swept up in the moment, her hands tangling in his soft hair, his gripping her bottom, holding her in place. Not that she wanted to escape; there was nowhere else she wanted to be. Unless it was in a bed, naked. Just the thought of Noah naked had her whimpering.

"I don't mind you two making out on my kitchen counter, but the least you could have done is let me know you there was food."

Mollie pulled back enough to look over Noah's shoulder and saw Jillian filling a plate. "Oops. Sorry. There are cookies, too, but you'd better grab one before Noah eats them all."

Noah rested his forehead on Mollie's, his breathing ragged. "Jillian, I'll buy you one hundred cookies if you leave right now."

Mollie put her hands on his chest, appreciating the hard pecs under his shirt even as she tried in vain to push him away. "Sorry, but it's her house. Now let me down so I can get my lunch."

Noah obliged, lifting her off the counter as if she weighed nothing, then letting her slide down the front of his body where she could feel the evidence of his frustration. She loved that she had that power over him, but the chemistry between them was going to make her crazy if they didn't take a step back and cool off. She had some photos she needed to edit; maybe it would be a good idea to take a break from each other for the afternoon, get some perspective. Otherwise she was liable to do something stupid, like seduce him past the line he'd drawn or confess her undying love. Which was insane, because they'd just met, and people didn't fall in love that fast. She just liked him. A lot. And, you know, wanted to jump his bones on the kitchen counter.

"You going to eat?" Jillian was already tucking into her food, sitting next to Noah at the same table they'd eaten the pie at the night before.

"Of course, do I ever turn down a meal?" She put a scoop of fish dip and a handful of crackers on her plate, along with some fruit. The cookies were gone, damn it. She plopped down on the other side of Jillian, who was barely picking at her food. "Hey, I thought you were hungry?"

"I thought so, too." She gave a rueful smile. "I just don't feel quite right. I thought a snack would help, but maybe not."

Mollie sat up straight, tension shooting down her spine. "Should we call the doctor? Does Nic know? Are you having contractions, headaches, what?"

Jillian held up a hand. "Whoa, slow down. No contractions. At least, I don't think so. I'm just tired and probably a little overheated. I spent most of the morning cleaning out the big flower garden over by the gazebo. Once I cool off a bit more, I'll be fine."

"You what?" Mollie dropped her fork with a clatter. "It's nearly a hundred degrees out there today, not to mention the humidity! You could have cooked that kid working outside like that."

Jillian smiled, but it didn't reach her eyes. "I doubt that. But I will admit it wore me out more than I realized. I promise to be more careful. Now, can I eat my lunch in peace or are you going to yell at me some more?"

"I don't know," Mollie answered honestly. The thought of something going wrong with Jillian's pregnancy had her insides all twisted up.

"Here, drink this." Noah set a large glass of ice water on the table in front of Jillian. "And when that's done, drink another. Dehydration can be serious during pregnancy."

Jillian shot Mollie a look, but didn't say anything other than a brief thank-you. She must be wondering how a single guy like Noah had a working knowledge of pregnancy, but she was too polite to ask. And Noah didn't look interested in sharing the details of his almost-baby. Yet another reminder why this vacation fling was destined to burn out. He was on the rebound in more ways than one, and if she didn't keep her feet under her she was going to wind up in a world of hurt. It was definitely time to put some distance between them.

She was about to say something about needing to leave when Jillian gasped, her knuckles turning white where she gripped the edge of the table.

"What, what is it?"

"I think… I think I had a contraction." Fear and pain tinged her voice. "But it's too early for contractions."

Mollie panicked for one small moment. Then she turned and ran down the hall, shouting for Nic, her feet slapping on the tile in rhythm with her jacked-up pulse.

"What?" Nic glared at her from his office doorway. "I'm trying to get some work done, if you don't mind."

"It's Jillian—she's in labor!"

Chapter Three

Noah shifted in a too-small plastic chair, watching Mollie pace the waiting room. He probably shouldn't even be here. He wasn't family, wasn't even really a friend, just a paying guest. But he'd given Mollie a ride, not wanting her to get behind the wheel in her agitated condition and knowing she'd be stranded at the hospital if she'd ridden with Jillian and Nic. An hour ago, he'd convinced her to grab a quick dinner in the cafeteria, but otherwise she'd spent the hours since they got here wearing a trench in the linoleum. It was enough to give him a headache. That, and the constant coming and going of families with new babies. A maternity-ward waiting area wasn't exactly on his top places to visit right now. Seeing the excitement was like having salt poured in a wound, one he wasn't sure how to mend. How did you get over losing a child you never really had?

Probably by moving on, getting back to who you were. Which wasn't a father or a family man. He didn't even have houseplants, never knowing when he'd decide to pick up and take off. He'd probably have messed it up anyway. But damn, he'd wanted to try.

The double doors at the end of the hall swung open, and a tired but grinning Nic walked out. "The contractions stopped. She's not dilated at all, and the baby's fine." He collapsed into the chair across from Noah. "She was just dehydrated and has what they called an irritable uterus. Not preterm labor."

"Oh, thank God." Mollie had tears in her eyes, but she forced a smile. "So everything is okay, really okay?"

"Everything is fine. They're going to keep her overnight, just so they can keep the IV going and monitor things, and she can go home in the morning. No bed rest or anything, but no more working in the heat, either."

Mollie pulled out her phone. "I'll call Cassie and let her know everything is okay. She wanted to come down but Alex was working and Emma was already in bed. And Nic, tell Jillian not to worry about work tomorrow. I'll cover for her."

"Thanks. She was already making noises about going straight to the clinic in the morning."

Mollie just rolled her eyes while listening to whoever was on the other end of the phone—her boss, Cassie, no doubt. It was good to see a group of friends sticking together and helping each other out, even if it meant he'd be on his own tomorrow. He'd kept to himself too much to make those kinds of connections in his own life, but when was he going to do what he could to change that? In the meantime, he'd get some sketching done and spend some time just chilling on the beach. If he really wanted to see Mollie, he could always take her to dinner or something. He could certainly wait until then.

He didn't even make it past lunch. Just before noon, he borrowed Nic's car and headed to the Paradise Animal Clinic, following the directions the couple had given him. He'd felt stupid asking for the favor, but that hadn't stopped him from doing it. Hopefully Mollie would be interested in going to lunch with him and not think he was some lovesick fool who couldn't stay away from her for more than a few hours. Even if it was the truth.

He pulled into a small lot in front of a cheery yellow building and told himself he was just a friend stopping by. A friend that had tossed and turned in bed all night thinking about her.

Inside he was met with the smell of disinfectant and wet dog, but at least the air was comfortably cool. An older woman was at the front desk, her gray hair cut in an efficient bob that matched the quick movement of her fingers across the keyboard in front of her. There was no one else in the waiting room, so he approached and waited for her to look up.

"Hello, can I help you?"

"Yes, I'm looking for Mollie. Is she available?"

"Who shall I say is asking for her?" The woman reminded him more of a butler than a receptionist, but Noah played along.

"Noah, Noah James. I was hoping to take her to lunch."

She frowned. "She didn't mention anything about that, but I'll let her know you're here."

Noah tried to look casual as he waited for her to fetch Mollie. He really should have called first. But that would have given her a chance to say no, and he wasn't risking that.

"Noah!" Mollie popped through a swinging door, looking all kinds of cute in scrubs and tennis shoes. "What are you doing here?" She halted midstep. "It isn't Jillian, is it?"

"Jillian's fine." Now he really felt like a jerk. "I just wanted to see if I could buy you lunch." *Because I missed you.*

She smiled and tilted her head, considering. "I'd like that, but I've got another half hour or so of work to do before I can leave. Can you come back in a bit? Or you could just hang out here, if you want. Might get boring, though."

"I'll stay. Just put me where I won't be in the way."

Forty-five minutes later, he was still leaning against a back wall in the main treatment area, and Mollie was scrubbing up to assist in surgery. The patient, a basset hound with a penchant for eating tennis balls, was already sedated, his remarkable X-ray hung up on the wall.

"I am so sorry," Mollie apologized for the third time. "But someone's got to stay, and with Jillian out, I'm it." She smiled self-consciously and lowered her voice. "I'm just hoping I don't mess up. Jillian's been training me to do more tech work, but this is my first surgery without her here."

"I'm sure you'll do fine." And he was sure. He'd been watching her work, and she had a rare combination of compassion and intelligence that made everyone around her more comfortable. He'd seen her easy connection with animals at the rehab center, but she seemed to get along with her human coworkers just as well. Even when the dog on the surgery table had given her a scare, his heart rate doing something loopy, she had kept her voice calm, her movements controlled. After dealing with the temperamental types so frequently found in the art world—not to mention Angela's near constant histrionics—Mollie's upbeat and competent calm was like a cool ocean breeze, refreshing and restoring.

"All right, let's fix this guy up before afternoon appointments start rolling in." Cassie, an athletic-looking strawberry blonde, called from a doorway. "Sorry about your lunch and for stealing your guide from you today."

"No worries. Is the dog going to be okay?"

Cassie nodded. "I think so. He's just going to be a bit out of sorts for a while."

Well, that was a feeling he could relate to.

Mollie rolled her neck, trying to relieve the stiffness. She'd been on her feet for almost twelve hours now, much of that time spent lifting or restraining animals that didn't understand she was trying to help them. Not to mention the stress of emergency surgery on that poor basset hound. Rambo was going to need to learn more discriminating dietary habits if he wanted to live out all his allotted doggie years.

"That's it, that's the last of them." Cassie hung up her stethoscope, a wan smile on her face. "Thanks again for coming in on your vacation. I couldn't have managed today without you. Janet can handle the front desk in a pinch, and I'm grateful she's willing to fill in...."

"But she's not about to wrangle a Dalmatian into the bathtub for a flea bath."

"No, definitely not." Cassie made a face.

Just the idea of the elderly former librarian doing such a thing had Mollie's lips twitching. She and Cassie were both a little slap happy at this point, exhaustion and low blood sugar taking their toll after a long, hard day. Lunch had been a package of peanuts scrounged from a desk drawer and a can of soda. Cassie had offered to share her protein shake, but Mollie had refused, knowing the pregnant veterinarian needed the nutrition to make it through the day. Now all she wanted was a hot meal and a good night's sleep. But first, she needed to stop by the inn. She told herself it was just to check on Jillian, but she needed to see Noah, too. She wanted to share her day with him, find out what he'd been up to. Just be with him.

A knock at the door startled her back into action. "I'll get it."

Cassie grimaced. "If it's an emergency, tell them I moved away."

As if the soft-hearted vet would ever turn away an animal in need. Bracing herself for another client, Mollie's jaw dropped when she opened the door. Stand-

ing there, like the answer to her prayers, was Noah,
two pizza boxes in his hands. Overwhelmed with gratitude, she pulled him in, planting a kiss right on his lips.
"You are my favorite person in the whole world, starting right now."

He waited for her to lock the door behind him. "A
pizza dinner and you're my biggest fan? What would
you do for surf and turf, I wonder?"

"Shut up and feed me. I'm starving." She read the
labels, one cheese, one with everything. Yum.

"Who was it?" Cassie asked, halfway back into her
white lab coat. Her eyes widened as Noah followed
Mollie into the room. "Our knight in shining armor,
apparently. And just in time. Even the dog kibble was
starting to look appetizing."

"Nic was coming into town to pick up some pizza
for Jillian, and I remembered that you said you wouldn't
have time for lunch. So I hitched a ride and figured I'd
add pizza delivery boy to my résumé."

"Well, bless you for thinking of it."

Conversation halted as they dug into the food, eating
off of pink paper plates that Mollie had found on top of
the staff refrigerator. For several minutes the only sound
was the occasional murmur of appreciation.

"Mommy?"

Cassie dropped her slice and wiped her hands. "I'm
coming." At Noah's confused look, she explained, "My
daughter. My husband drops her off before he starts his
night shift with the sheriff's department." She went
back up front, returning a minute later with the little
girl, a miniature version of herself.

Mollie gave the girl a hug, and then introduced her. "Emma, this is Mr. James. He's staying at the Sandpiper with Mr. Nic and Miss Jillian."

The little girl nodded, her eyes on the food behind him. "Did you bring the pizza? Can I have some, too? I love pizza."

"Emma, it isn't polite to—"

Noah brushed aside Cassie's concern. "Of course you can. It would be rude of me not to share. Which kind do you want?"

"I'll get it for her." Mollie swept the child up into her lap, and slid a piece of plain cheese onto a clean plate. "There you go, cuddle bug." Mollie kept an arm around Emma's waist while she ate, partly to keep her from toppling out of the chair, partly because she liked snuggling the sweet girl. Back when Cassie had been a single mom, Mollie had spent a lot of time babysitting. She'd thought she was doing it just to help out Cassie, but now that Emma had a new stepfather in the picture and two sets of doting grandparents, Mollie was finding she really missed her time with the munchkin.

She always had enjoyed being around children, but that didn't mean she was looking to have her own. At least not anytime soon. Maybe after she'd made a name for herself, really gotten her career going, she could consider it. With the right guy. Her gaze strayed to Noah, her heart thumping a resounding *yes* at the idea. But her biological clock would have to reset itself, because her career trajectory was currently flatlined. It would be a long time before she reached a level where she could feel comfortable shifting her focus from it.

And that was okay. She had her friends, she had Baby and she was having an amazing but short-term fling with a famous artist. She certainly didn't need a committed relationship or a child to be fulfilled; that was the trap her mother had fallen into. No, she'd enjoy being the babysitter, and have her fun with Noah, and keep her eye on the prize. She couldn't afford to get sidetracked, no matter how tempting the idea was.

Mollie's feet were dragging by the time she and Noah got back to the Sandpiper. Clomping up the steps with all the grace of a seasick elephant, she forced herself to keep moving.

"You know, you don't have to walk me in. You should go home and get some rest. We were all up late last night, and you've been on your feet all day."

Mollie shook her head. "I'll go home as soon as I check on Jillian." Last night had been terrifying—no way was she going to be able to sleep until she saw with her own eyes that everything was okay. They found Jillian in the office she shared with Nic, squinting at what looked like a brochure template on her laptop. Next to her was a large water bottle with the words *Drink Me* scrawled across it. Courtesy of Nic, no doubt. Relief washed over her, Jillian looked as good as ever. Glowing, even. Crossing the room, she gave her friend a hug. "You know, if you wanted a day off, you could have just asked. No need for the drama." She swallowed past the lump in her throat and sat on the edge of a chair. "Seriously though, you look much better."

"I should. I slept until noon, and I've had enough fluids to float the *Titanic*. I swear my feet are going to start sloshing when I walk." She closed her laptop. "Thanks again for covering for me today. I appreciate it. I promise not to let myself get run-down like that again."

"You'd better not. You scared the crap out of us last night."

Jillian sobered. "I know, I don't think Nic's over it yet. He wouldn't even let me go out to get the mail, insisted on doing it himself. Which reminds me, someone called here looking for you." She peeled a pink sticky note off of her desktop and held it out for Mollie.

"For me? Who would call me here?"

"I don't know, but he asked you to call back, said it was important."

The name, George Reeves, was unfamiliar, and the area code was from out of state. Curiouser and curiouser. She glanced at the clock. It was almost eight; was that too late to call? Of course, if it was important, waiting until tomorrow could be a mistake. Choosing action over inaction, she pulled her cell phone from her pants pocket and dialed.

A few nerve-racking minutes of conversation later and her hands were shaking so hard it took her three tries to turn off her phone.

"What, what is it?" Jillian's concerned voice cut through the roaring in her ears. "Is everything okay?"

Mollie nodded, speechless for the first time in her life.

Noah, looking way too smug, left his perch against the wall and took the phone out of her still trembling hands. "So, are you going to tell us what he had to say?"

"Did you do this?" He must have. It was the only thing that made sense.

"Do what? You still haven't told us what he said. Or who he was, for that matter." Jillian looked from Mollie to Noah. "Can one of you fill me in?"

"That was the owner of a gallery in Atlanta. He saw my work and wants to include it in an upcoming show." Even saying it out loud it still didn't seem real. "He wants to hang my photographs in a gallery. In Atlanta." Nerves tossed her insides like waves after a storm. "Could this be some kind of a hoax?"

Noah smiled like a kid given a second summer vacation. "It's no hoax. George Reeves is the real deal. He's displayed some of my stuff—sold some of it for a good price, too."

Pieces clicked together, and her excitement began to ebb. "So it *was* you. You asked him to do this, as a favor?" She shot out of the chair, pulling her hands away. She didn't want to be touching him right now. Hell, she didn't want to be in the same room with him right now. "Is this some kind of trick, a way to get into my pants? Give me a pity showing, and I'll be so grateful I'll have sex with you?"

"No, of course not."

"Then what, some kind of weird payback because I was nice to you? Because I don't need your pity. Or your favors. I'm going to make it one day, and it's going to be based on my talent. And nothing but my talent." She'd heard of red-hot rage, and now she knew what it meant. Anger burned through her, narrowing her vision and heating her blood. She wouldn't be surprised if she could actually breathe fire.

"Mollie, be reasonable—"

"Reasonable?" She laughed, a bitter, hollow sound. "Oh, Noah, you really don't know me at all, do you? I'm known for a lot of things, but reasonable isn't one of them. A reasonable, sensible girl wouldn't have gone to dinner with you when you were drunk. A reasonable woman wouldn't have offered to be your tour guide on her vacation, or let you kiss her in her friend's kitchen. So you can shove your reasonable up your famous ass." Pivoting, she stormed out of the room.

"Wait, Mollie!"

She ignored him and kept going, down the hall, through the lobby and out the door. She didn't stop until she hit sand, kicking her shoes and socks off on the way. Damn him, she was crying, and she was not a crier. But for a minute there she'd thought this was it; this was going to be her big break. More than that, though, she'd thought Noah understood her, that he got what it was like to have a dream. Obviously not. She was just some chick that he could buy off. No wonder he didn't have many friends, if this was how he treated them.

The glow of a flashlight gave away his presence, and she considered trying to outrun him. But he knew where she lived, and she had a feeling he could be persistent. He'd arranged a gallery showing just to impress her. Who knew what he'd do next?

Noah was breathing hard by the time he reached Mollie. He was in good shape, but running on sand was harder than it looked. The exertion wasn't the real reason his pulse was pounding, though; the betrayal in Mollie's eyes had done that. He'd messed up, big time. He should have asked her before doing anything. Now she thought he was a manipulative bastard, and he didn't blame her.

"What do you want?" Mollie was sitting in the sand, her knees drawn up to her chest like a child. He dimmed the flashlight, letting his eyes adjust to the moonlit night.

"I want to apologize. I shouldn't have acted without your permission."

"Damn straight." Her chin jutted out, but he could still see the tracks her tears had made on her face.

"But you should also know I didn't buy you a spot in the show. I didn't even know he was going to offer you one."

She looked up, confusion clouding her eyes. "Then how? Why?"

"I sent him the link to the rehab center's website, the page with your photos on it. I knew they were good when I saw them on the wall, but I wanted George's opinion. I figured he could maybe hook you up with a dealer, stir up some interest. I had no idea he was going to book you into a show."

"You didn't?"

He shook his head. "No, but I should have. You're really good. I thought maybe I was biased, given how I feel about you, but obviously George thinks so, too."

She frowned, looking up at him, her eyes demanding a straight answer. "You don't think he's doing this just as a favor to you?"

"A favor? George Reeves doesn't do favors for anyone. Trust me, if he wants your work, it's because he thinks you have talent. Period."

She sniffed, and he realized she'd been crying this whole time, silently so he wouldn't hear. Hell. He sat down on the sand beside her, pulling her into his lap where he could feel her quiet sobs. "Don't cry, okay? If you don't want to do the show, I'll just tell him to buzz off."

She punched his shoulder and pulled away from him. "Don't you dare! I'm not crying because I'm mad anymore, I'm crying because it's a dream come true."

"Say what?"

"Happy tears, you idiot. Now shut up and kiss me, before you ruin it,"

Now he understood. He palmed the back of her head and pulled her in, his lips seeking hers by the light of the full moon. Slowly, knowing how close he'd come to losing her trust, he kept the kiss gentle. He sampled rather than devoured, nipping at her lips and then soothing them with a flick of his tongue. She whimpered and wrapped her arms around his neck, her fingers tracing patterns along his scalp. Kissing her more firmly, he teased at the seam of her lips, then took the kiss deeper when she opened for him. Seconds turned into minutes, and the crash of the waves was replaced by the pounding of his own heart. She squirmed in his lap, spiking his desire. Lifting her, he turned and laid her on the sand, tracing the lines of her face with the pad of his thumb.

"You're beautiful, you know that? Prettier than anything should be."

"You're not so bad yourself." She tried to sit up, but he stilled her with another kiss. "Let me just look at you for a minute. I want to remember this. I want to remember you with the stars reflected in your eyes."

"Because you're going to leave."

Yeah, he was. But he didn't want to. Not now, and maybe not ever. "You could come with me. To Atlanta."

It was a crazy idea.

But it didn't feel crazy.

She shook her head. "You can't expect me to just pick up and follow you out of the state after knowing you less than a week."

"No, I guess not." So much for that idea.

"But I could come visit you." She offered a vulnerable smile. "I'll be going to Atlanta anyway, for the show. I could stay for a few extra days, let you show me around this time."

It was a start. When she ran out of the inn, he thought he'd lost her, but she was giving him a second chance. They were together for now, and they would be again, on his home turf. "You've got a deal."

Chapter Four

Mollie felt nearly boneless, the sun and sand having once again erased all the tension from her body. Hard to believe she'd been such a basket case just last night. Turning her head to the side, she could see Noah in a similar state of relaxation, spread out on his beach towel looking like every girl's fantasy. The sun had burnished his olive skin to a dark bronze, and his low slung trunks showed off what seemed like acres of lean muscle. Needing to touch, she reached out and traced the top ridge of his six-pack.

"If you keep touching me like that, I'm going to have to roll over to keep from embarrassing myself."

Intrigued, she let her hand drift lower, following the line of hair that started at his navel and disappeared under the edge of his bathing suit.

Noah's breath shot out in a hiss. Then, without warning he scooped her up, throwing her over his shoulder as he stood.

"What are you doing?" She kicked a bit, feeling silly with her head hanging halfway down his back, her only view his butt and the sand beneath his feet. Which, come to think of it, wasn't a bad one, after all. Giggling, she squirmed again, and he just clamped down on her legs more firmly, his step never faltering as he hit the water's edge. "Put me down."

"Okay, but you asked for it."

He dunked them both, letting her slide down his body as they sunk beneath the waves. Weightlcss, she held her breath, surfacing at the same time he did. Liquid sluiced down his face, his eyes simmering with heat despite the icy water surrounding them. But even that intensity was balanced by a cheeky grin. She loved that he could be sexy and playful at the same time. She loved a lot of things about him, actually.

"What's that smile about?" He wiped her dripping hair off her brow and then landed a gentle kiss on her upturned lips.

"I'm just happy." She was a naturally upbeat person, but today she felt like she was floating.

"About anything in particular?"

"Hmm, maybe," she teased. "I mean, it is a beautiful day."

"Uh-huh. Anything else?"

"Well, I don't know if you've heard, but I have a gallery showing coming up."

He nodded gravely. "That does sound familiar. Sure there isn't anything else?"

"I can't think of anything." He moved to dunk them again and she laughed, "Fine, yes, I'm also happy that I met you, and that I'm going to get to see you again, in Atlanta."

"That's better. I was starting to wonder if you were getting sick of me."

"Not yet. Of course, you're here for another two days, so maybe by then…" She sobered at the thought. Two days wasn't very long, and the show in Atlanta wasn't for another month. Of course, she'd be back to her regular life then—going to school, working, spending time with her family.

"Oh my gosh, I forgot about my family!"

"What about them?"

"I totally forgot to call and tell them about the invitation to the show. I should stop by there and show them the contract. Maybe that will prove to them that my photography isn't just a silly hobby."

"Well, then, let's go see them. You signed off on everything this morning, right?" She nodded. She'd spent most of the morning filling out the forms the gallery had sent over and oohing and aahing over their website. Noah had finally come by and dragged her out of the house, promising she'd have plenty of time to sift through it all later. They'd eaten Cuban sandwiches at Alejandro's again and then spent the afternoon on the beach stealing kisses and acting like tourists.

"Then we might as well celebrate, now that it's official. I bet Nic keeps some decent champagne. I'll grab a bottle and we can all toast to your career."

"Um, okay." She hadn't taken a guy to meet her parents since high school; this was going to be interesting. And even though Noah probably wasn't thinking of it that way, her parents would.

"You don't have to come, if you don't want to. I could just run by, then come back afterwards."

He shook his head. "No way am I missing out on this celebration. We'll go together."

She swallowed, not seeing a way out. Oh well, her parents would just have to deal. "Let's head up and get changed, then. I don't think I'll be able to pull off a professional vibe if I'm in a bikini."

They ran up to the Sandpiper so Noah could get cleaned up and then headed to Mollie's house. She showered quickly and changed into a soft blue tank and a pair of tan capris. Not exactly high fashion, but compared to her normal cutoffs, it was a step up. She felt good in it, and if Noah's look of appreciation could be trusted, she looked good too. She'd even taken the time to blow-dry her hair and put on some makeup while Noah busied himself filling Baby's food and water bowls. Having a doggy door meant she didn't have to worry about letting Baby in and out, but he did expect his meals delivered on time and in sufficient quantity.

"All set?" Noah was leaning against her counter, looking for all the world as if he belonged right there in her kitchen, in her life. But as comfortable as it felt having him around, she needed to keep her head in the game. Dating him was one thing; making him a permanent part of her life was another. She'd gotten a toe-hold on success, but it was a long climb to the top. She needed to focus and stay nimble if she was going to make it in the art world. Her career had to come first, not a man.

She gripped the champagne Noah had brought in one hand and her signed contract in the other. "Ready as I'll ever be."

Noah watched the sky turn colors outside the car window as Mollie silently navigated the streets of her hometown. She'd been quiet ever since he suggested going to her parents' house. Did she think this was some kind of relationship milestone he was pushing on her? He wasn't trying to make a statement; he just wanted to be there for her, especially if her parents weren't as excited as she hoped. Heck, he wanted to be with her whenever something important happened. But how could he say that, given everything she'd said about avoiding long-term relationships? He needed to give her the space she needed and hope that in time she realized he would never stand in the way of her dreams. It wasn't much of a plan, but it was the only one he had.

Mollie stopped the car in front of a modest but well-kept single story home. A large oak tree dominated the yard, shading the manicured lawn. A hedge of hibiscus flowers bordered the driveway, and he could smell jasmine in the air. Mollie got out, and he followed her up a cobblestone path to the front door. She briefly knocked, then surprised him by walking right in.

"They don't lock the front door?"

"No one around here does, at least not during the day. Paradise isn't exactly a high-crime area."

Maybe not, but he'd lived in big cities too long to be comfortable with that level of openness. "You lock your door, though, right?" The idea of someone being able to walk in on her made his blood run cold.

She shrugged. "When I remember. But don't worry—I've got Baby. No one's going to bother me."

True, a dog that size was probably better protection than any dead bolt. He was just being paranoid, hating the idea that he'd be leaving in a couple days and she'd be here alone.

"Mom, Dad, are you home?" Mollie led them through a white-tiled foyer, past a sunken living room to their left and into an eat-in kitchen that looked out onto a small family room. A tall, slender woman with brunette hair pulled into a sleek ponytail stood at the counter chopping vegetables for a salad. Obviously Mollie's mother, she had the same ethereal grace and slight build as her daughter. Only the faint lines around her eyes and a few streaks of gray in her hair kept her from looking more like an older sister than the matriarch of the family.

"Mollie, what a surprise. I didn't know you were coming by. Are you and your friend staying for dinner?"

"Um, I don't think so. I just wanted to stop by and tell you and Dad something. Is he here?"

"He's in his office. Dani's in there with him. She wanted his advice about a new case she's working on. Why don't you go drag them out of there, or they'll be talking opening arguments for hours."

"Sure. Noah, I'll be right back. Oh, and this is my mom, Anna Post. Mom, this is Noah James. He's a friend of Nic's and is staying at the Sandpiper this week."

"Nice to meet you, Noah."

"The pleasure is all mine."

Mollie stepped around her mother, stealing a slice of red pepper as she walked by. Sticking her head into the hallway on the opposite side of the kitchen, she said something he couldn't quite hear, then turned back. "They're coming."

She paced back to him, and he almost reached for her hand to reassure her. Not a good move. If she'd wanted to advertise their relationship, she wouldn't have introduced him as Nic's friend.

A movement in the hall alerted him to the arrival of the rest of the family. Mr. Post was broad where his wife was slender, his shoulders nearly taking up the entire doorway. He was average height, in good shape, and had a full head of salt and pepper hair. Behind him was Dani, an athletic blonde who seemed to have inherited her father's strong physique as well as his interest in the law.

"Hey, sis, did you come by to mooch some of Mom's food? I know that's why I'm here." She stopped in her tracks, eyeing Noah like he was another menu item. "Who's the beefcake?"

Mollie rolled her eyes, then plucked a cherry tomato from the cutting board. "That's Noah. Noah, the smart aleck over there is my sister, Dani. You'd think a lawyer would have better people skills, but somehow she keeps winning cases."

The sisters' looks and lifestyles might be worlds apart, but they obviously had a similar sense of humor. And, he saw as Mollie swiped another tomato and tossed it to Dani, a close bond. "Nice to meet you Dani, and you, Mr. Post."

Dani nodded, her mouth full, but Mollie's father came over and offered his hand. "Nice to meet you, too, Noah…?"

"Noah James, sir." The man's handshake was firm, but not so strong it could be considered an attempt to intimidate.

"Are you two staying for dinner?"

Mollie stepped forward, taking control of the situation. "No, Dad. We came by because I have some news."

"News?" Dani's eyes widened.

"Yes." Mollie squared her shoulders, her eyes shining with pride. "I was offered my first gallery showing in Atlanta." She held up the contract in one hand, and the champagne in the other. "So I thought we should celebrate."

"That's awesome!" Dani high-fived her sister, then began pulling champagne flutes out of a kitchen cabinet. "So, does this mean people are going to buy your pictures?"

"Maybe, I hope so." Mollie started wrestling with the wire cage on the champagne bottle.

"Hold on, slow down here." Mollie's father furrowed his brow. "How did this happen? Are you sure it's legit?

I've heard of scams, where they make artists pay for a spot and then it turns out the gallery never existed."

"Dad, yes, it's real." Mollie's shoulders sunk, hurt tingeing her voice. "But if the idea of me having real talent is so hard to believe, ask Noah. He knows the owner."

She should have known they'd react like this. Why couldn't they just be happy for her? At least Dani had congratulated her, rather than suggesting it was a scam like her father had. And Mom had that concerned look on her face she wore whenever one of her kids got into trouble.

"The gallery is legit, as is the offer." Noah took her hand, squeezing it in encouragement. He'd only known her a few days and was ready to stand by her. Why couldn't her parents give her the same kind of support?

"Honey, I'm sorry. I didn't mean to doubt your abilities. It's just out of the blue, is all. How did this happen?"

"They saw my work, and they liked it." It stung that her own abilities weren't enough to convince them, but maybe explaining Noah's connection to the art world would help. "Noah's shown some of his sculptures there, and he contacted the owner."

"What sculptures?" Her mom wiped her hands on a dish cloth and went to stand by her husband.

"Noah works as a metal sculptor. His last piece was featured in *Architectural Digest*. You can look up him online if you don't believe me."

Dani pulled her phone out and looked like she was doing just that.

"I thought you said Noah was a friend of Nic's?" Her mom blinked in confusion. "Now he's some famous artist?"

"I did a piece for Caruso Hotels a while back. That's when I met Nic. And yes, I've been lucky enough to be very successful with my art. But I didn't call in any favors, if that's what you're thinking. I just sent the owner a link to some of the photos she's done for the animal rehab center. He liked what he saw and thought she'd do well in his upcoming show. Mollie got this on her own merits. You should be proud of her."

Her dad cleared his throat. "Well, of course we're proud of her. It's not that. We just want to make sure she's thinking it all through." He nodded at her mother. "Right, honey?"

"Of course. It sounds impressive. But what about school and work? Can you just pick up and go to Atlanta like that?"

She held back a sigh, knowing that keeping calm was the only way to win them over. "It's a month away, and I'll only be gone a few days." Maybe longer, if she wanted to spend extra time with Noah. "I'm sure Cassie will give me the time off, and I can talk to my professors about it ahead of time. But I'm not going to let this opportunity go by, no matter what."

Her father jumped back in; they made quite the tag team, those two. "I know you want to do this. It's an honor, I'm sure. But we just don't want you to get sidetracked, that's all. Photography is enjoyable, and it's great that you might sell some of your work. But you need to remember that art isn't something you can count on, long-term."

"Not if I never try, it isn't." She blinked against the tears that had started to form. "And maybe you're right. Maybe I'm not good enough to make a career out of it. But the only way I'll find out is if I do my best and it isn't good enough. This show could open doors for me, get me noticed. Maybe I could even get some magazine work, I don't know. But I'm going to find out. I'm going to go to Atlanta, and I'm going to follow every lead I can and learn as much as I can. And I'm going to stay in school, not because it makes you happy, but because I want to learn more and get better at what I do. Which isn't law or accounting or any of those practical things you keep trying to push on me. I'm sorry, I can't be who you want me to be—I can't be another Dani."

Well, now she'd done it. Her father looked ready to argue, but her mom just looked hurt.

Dani, however, was laughing. "Well, thank God for that! I'm not looking for a clone. In fact, pass me that bottle, Noah. I want to make a toast."

Noah popped the cork with a practiced ease and handed her the champagne, watching her fill the glasses with an amused smile.

"To my sister, the photographer. May she remember us little people when she's famous one day."

Mollie gave a brittle smile. Thank heavens her sister stood by her. Growing up, she'd never lorded her own success over Mollie, but had treated her as an equal.

But Dani's support wasn't enough to balance out her parents' doubts.

As she sipped what was probably very expensive champagne, all she could taste was disappointment. She'd really thought this might finally impress her parents and get them to understand how important photography was to her. But it wasn't enough. It probably never would be. Her father wanted her to do something more lucrative, and her mother wanted her to have stability. What no one seemed to care about was what she wanted. Well, other than Dani.

And Noah, she realized. He'd braved this awkward family drama with grace and had defended her without bulldozing her. Her parents might be trying to control her, but he hadn't, not once. Instead he had encouraged her to chase her dreams. Even knowing that meant putting her career ahead of him.

As much as Noah had worried this might happen, it was obvious Mollie had expected a different sort of reaction from her parents. He could almost understand their concerns, probably from hearing similar ones expressed by his own father year after year. But where he had rebelled, he could see Mollie was just devastated. She had a closeness with her family that he'd never quite managed, and that gave her parents' words more weight. Weight that was crushing her right in front of his eyes.

"I think we'd better leave you all to your dinner. It was nice meeting you." He wrapped an arm around Mollie, her bare arms like ice against his skin.

"You don't have to go—"

"Yes, they do." Dani interrupted her mother, refilling the glass she'd already drained. "They wanted to celebrate, so let them go do that."

Mollie found his hand, holding it with a death grip that belied her calm tone. "Mom, Dad, I appreciate your concern but I don't think there is anything else to say. I'll send you a postcard from Atlanta."

On that note Noah guided Mollie out of the house, wondering what it was between parents and their children that made everything so hard. He'd certainly never managed to see eye to eye on much with his own, but he'd thought that was because of their strained relationship. The pendulum swung the other way in Mollie's family, but the damage was just as great.

Outside he held the car door for Mollie. As she set her purse on the center console, she frowned, then quickly sifted through the contents. "Hell's bells. I think I left the contract on the counter inside." Her head fell back against the seat, her eyes closed. "I do not want to go back in there."

He didn't blame her after that scene. "I'll go get it, and you wait here."

"Thanks. I just don't want to get into it again with them, you know?"

"I know." He closed the car door gently and jogged back up to the house. Her father answered the door.

"Mollie forgot the contract—I told her I'd grab it while she started the car."

Moving aside, the older man let him by. "I feel like I should apologize."

"You don't need to, not to me. Mollie's the one that's hurting right now."

"Fair enough. But let me at least try to explain. Please."

Noah walked to the counter and picked up the contract, then nodded. The man clearly cared for his daughter, even if he wasn't doing a great job of showing it.

Her father sighed, looking older than he had just a few minutes ago. "It's not that we don't appreciate Mollie's talent or care about her feelings. It's just that we know how hard it can be to make a living doing something so…impractical."

The last sculpture Noah had sold probably cost more than this guy's mortgage, but pointing that out wasn't going to help the situation. "There aren't any guarantees when it comes to a career in art, but respectfully, sir, that's true of many things. There isn't much in life that's a sure thing."

Mollie's mother, who'd been quietly stirring something on the stove, broke in. "It's not just about the money. We didn't raise Mollie to be a snob. When I was a dancer, it wasn't the size of my paycheck that was an issue. It was never knowing if the next part would be your last, never knowing what was around the corner. The uncertainty of it all can wear you down and the isolation can be crippling. It's a hard life, and it can be a lonely one. I don't want that for my daughter."

"With all due respect, ma'am, I think that's her choice to make. She's a grown woman, smarter and stronger than most."

Her father nodded slowly. "We know that. We just want her to be happy."

"I believe you. But giving up her dream isn't going to make her happy, and neither is going against your wishes. If you make her choose, she's going to be miserable either way."

Which was why he was going to be damned sure he didn't put her in the same situation.

"If you want her to be happy, you have to trust her, that she knows what she wants, risks and all. It might not be what you want, but it doesn't have to be, if you love her. Now, if you'll excuse me, I've got a celebration to save."

He let himself out and found Mollie nervously drumming her fingers on the steering wheel. She started the car and cast an anxious glance back at the house. "Were they okay?"

"Yeah. They're fine, just confused. What about you—are you okay?"

"I am now." She took a deep breath, the tension visibly leaving her body. "Thanks for coming with me. It helped, knowing you were there, that you believed in me."

"Anytime." He always wanted to be there, to have her back. Maybe now was the time to tell her. "Listen, I know you said you don't have room in your life for a relationship, that you don't want to sacrifice your goals for love. But just because your mom gave up dancing when she got married and had kids doesn't mean it always has to work that way. Having a family doesn't have to mean losing yourself or giving up who you are."

Mollie's face paled under the yellow glow of the street lights. "You say that now, but—"

"But nothing." He waited until she'd stopped for a red light, the streets deserted in either direction. Reaching out, he stroked her cheek before gently turning her fact towards him, needing her to see his sincerity. "I didn't plan for this to happen, and there are a million reasons it can't work. But I believe in being honest. And the honest truth is, I'm falling in love with you."

She couldn't have heard that right. "You're what?"

"I'm falling in love with you." Any hope that he wasn't serious was dashed by the heated look in his eyes. "I didn't mean for it to happen, if that helps."

She didn't know whether to laugh or cry. He was crazy; there was no other explanation. "But you're on your honeymoon. A week ago, you were going to get married to another woman, for the love of all things holy." White-knuckling the steering wheel, she made the last turn onto her street and pulled into the driveway. Shutting the car off, she turned in her seat to face him. She needed to set him straight, and fast. "So there is no way you could be in love with me."

"But I am." His eyes sought hers. "I know the timing is awkward."

She snorted. "Gee, you think?"

"But that doesn't change how I feel. I think I fell for you that first day when I saw you on the steps of the Sandpiper. You're beautiful, and talented, and you go out of your way to make everyone around you happy. You're the most amazing person I've ever met, and I don't want to just be some guy that you met on vacation."

"I said I'd visit when I'm in Atlanta." Why couldn't that be enough for him?

"I want more."

His eyes had gone dark, his voice thick with emotion. Part of her—okay, a big part—wanted to say the words he wanted to hear, but she couldn't. She was finally getting her career on track, and she owed it to herself to stick with her promises. If she compromised her future to be with him, she'd regret it forever. "Noah… I can't. I'm sorry, I just can't. In a few years, maybe…"

Pain flashed in his eyes, but he didn't argue. "Don't be sorry. You didn't do anything wrong. I'm the one pushing when I have no right to. You told me up front that you weren't looking for anything serious."

"So where does that leave us?"

"We go back to the way things were. No strings, no pressure."

A tightness eased in her chest. She couldn't commit to him, but she wasn't ready to say goodbye, either, at least not yet. "I liked things the way they were." She licked her lips and watched his gaze follow her tongue.

"You did, huh?" His tone was all smoke and whiskey, his features dark and dangerous in the moonlight. And dangerous was exactly what he was.

Before she had time to form her next thought, he'd crossed the tiny distance between the seats, his hand anchored in her hair as his mouth came crashing down on hers. Their other kisses had been passionate; this time he was possessing, nearly bruising as he probed and then penetrated, tangling his tongue with hers. She shifted on the seat, needing more contact, but trapped by the gearshift and center console.

As if sensing her frustration, he undid her seat belt and lifted her up and over into his lap. The angle of the kiss changed, his mouth trailing down her neck, his tongue sending tiny shocks down her spine. She could feel how much he wanted her as she wiggled in his lap, trying to maneuver in the narrow confines. "You were right." She bit off a moan as he bit her earlobe. "I do need a bigger car. Much bigger."

"So you're saying size matters?"

"Definitely." From what she could feel, he had nothing to worry about in that department. "I'm thinking an SUV. A big one."

"How about we just move inside before your neighbors call the cops on us and Cassie's husband has to arrest me?"

"Neighbors? Oh, right." Her windows weren't even tinted; they'd been totally exposed and she hadn't once thought about anyone seeing them. He had a way of making her forget everything but him. Not good, not good at all. Even if it felt wonderful.

He opened the passenger door for her and she climbed out of his lap, banging her head on the roof of the car. "Damn it!"

"Are you okay?" She rubbed her head and nodded, but she was anything but okay. This was supposed to have been a fling, just a little fooling around before going back to real life. He could work off his rebound energy and she could have some fun before doubling down on her goals. But no, he had to go and say the L-word. Even worse, she'd almost said it back. Then what? As tempting as it was to just go with her feelings, she had to think of her future. If she sacrificed her dreams for him, she'd end up resenting him later. And she wouldn't do that, not to him and not to herself.

Besides, he couldn't really be in love with her. He might think he was, but no doubt he'd be over her by the time his flight landed in Atlanta.

Putting her key in the lock, she opened the door and absently patted Baby when he greeted her. Soon it would be just him and her again.

Suddenly exhausted, she considered their dinner options. "How about I call for pizza, and you find us a movie to watch? I think that's as much of a celebration as I can handle right now."

"That sounds perfect. Just no anchovies." He pressed a kiss to the top of her head and some of the tension of the last hour melted away. He wasn't going to press her; it was going to be fine. They'd have some food, cuddle on the couch, and just enjoy the time they had left. She could do this.

Chapter Five

Noah flipped through the on-demand movie options, looking for a comedy. Or an action movie. Just not a romance. The last thing he needed was to remind Mollie he was in love with her. She'd made it perfectly clear that she wasn't ready to settle down or make a commitment. She had a career to build, and he knew more than most the amount of time and dedication that took. It wasn't that many years ago that he'd been her place, just starting out. He'd had to focus 100 percent on his art to get that first big sale, and then he'd spent the next several years scrambling to keep the momentum going. Work-life balance wasn't something he'd had time to worry about, so how could he blame her for not wanting to take it on?

He couldn't.

She'd been right to shut him down. They were in two different places, going different directions. Which meant, if he really loved her, he'd let her go.

They had tonight and tomorrow, and then he'd be headed back to Atlanta and regular life, one without Mollie. The thought was like a physical pain, but there was nothing to be done about it, other than enjoy what time they had left.

Two hours later, they were curled up on the couch watching a second-rate movie, a half-eaten pizza on the coffee table in front of them. Or rather, he was watching the movie—Mollie had passed out before the first chase scene. In her sleep she was even more achingly beautiful, her long lashes making perfect half-moons against her creamy skin. Careful not to wake her, he stretched for the remote and turned off the movie, a blank screen replacing the rolling credits. He should leave and head back to his borrowed bed at the Sandpiper. But tonight was his last night in Paradise, and if he had the chance to hold her he was going to take it.

Sliding down, he tucked one arm under his head and rested the other across her chest. He could feel her heart beat, ticking away as if marking the time they had left. His own squeezed in response. No, he wasn't leaving tonight. He'd grab every last minute he could.

He lay there a long time, just listening to her breathe before he finally drifted off into a restless kind of sleep. Sometime later, he woke to an elbow digging into his ribcage. Eyes closed, he tried to shift, realizing too late that the couch was a lot smaller than his bed back at the inn. He hit the floor with a solid thunk, Mollie landing on top of him.

"Ow!"

"Are you okay?" He smoothed his hands down her body, not sure what he was even feeling for.

"Yeah. I just bit my lip."

His eyes had adjusted enough to the low light for him to see her gingerly touch her lip with the tips of her fingers. Still on top of him, her face was only inches away from his. Lifting his head he gently kissed the spot she'd touched. "Better?"

"Mmm-hmm." She nearly purred her agreement, and every sleeping cell in his body woke up, alert. She leaned in, brushing her mouth across his, and that was it—he was lost.

He rolled them, bracing himself above her, his hands on either side of her face. Her eyes were heavy with sleep and desire, her lips parted and her breathing heavy. She was by far the sexiest thing he'd ever seen, and he had to have her. Now. Here. Tonight. Nothing else mattered anymore; there was just the two of them in the silence of the night.

As if she'd sensed his decision or just reached the same conclusion on her own, she worked her hands under his shirt, her hands skating along his spine as she tried to free him from the fabric without breaking the kiss. Taking control, he shifted his weight to one hand and tore the shirt off with the other. A sigh of appreciation escaped her lips before she moved to explore more of his now bare skin.

Needing to even the playing field, he edged up the

silky tank she wore, the sight of her lacy black bra pushing him one step closer to the edge. He hadn't been this worked up since his teenage rumblings in the backseat of a car, but with Mollie everything was more intense, more real. "If you're going to tell me to stop, tell me now." His voice sounded unrecognizable, more growl than human speech. She reduced him to bare instinct, the desire to mate and possess throbbing through his blood.

She wrapped one long, lean leg around his waist, holding him to her. "Don't you dare stop."

That was all he needed to hear. He found her mouth again, suckling her bottom lip while his hands went for the clasp of her bra. She arched her back to give him better access, pressing her barely covered breasts up as if in offering. He slid the fastener free, but didn't pull the material away. She was a masterpiece, and he planned to study her inch by glorious inch. He licked along the ridge of her collarbone, then stifled her gasp of pleasure with another kiss.

At first he thought the ringing in his ears was from his skyrocketing blood pressure. But the sound continued, high pitched and utterly unwelcome.

Mollie's small hands pushed against his bare chest. "You should get that."

Cursing whatever phone gods he'd pissed off he got to his feet and snatched the ringing device off of the coffee table. Glancing at the display, he saw an unfamiliar number with an Atlanta area code and out of habit hit the speakerphone icon. "What?" Whoever it was better have a damned good reason for calling after midnight. Not to mention interrupting the most erotic moment of his life.

A saccharine sweet voice responded, "Is this Mr. Noah James?"

"It is."

"I'm calling from St. Luke's Hospital. We have a patient here, a Ms. Angela Garner. She's in labor and she's asking for you."

Anger coiled in his gut. "Why the hell should I care?"

"She listed you as the father of her unborn child."

"That can't be right. I'm afraid you've made a mistake."

"There's no mistake, sir. The paternity results are right here in the chart."

Mollie could hear every word of Noah's conversation, the sound carrying clearly in the still dark apartment. Tears stung her eyes, but she didn't have the right to cry. She should never have gotten involved with him, and half-naked rolling on the floor certainly counted as involved. Turning her back on him, she pulled down her shirt and then refastened her bra with shaking hands. How could she have let this happen? Getting caught up in the moment was no excuse. Not that her jumbled-up feelings were the issue right now. What mattered was getting him to Atlanta. He was going to be a father. Another woman just had his child. He should be at her side, no matter what had happened between them.

Steeling herself, she stole a glance at Noah. He was staring at the phone in his hand as if he couldn't understand what it was for. She took it from him and spoke to the woman on the other end of the line, writing down the details on the back of a napkin. Hanging up, she handed it back to him.

"Mollie...." His voice trailed off, his expression lost. "I have to—"

"I know." That he needed to leave was the one thing she did understand. "I'll drive you to the airport. I can have Jillian ship your things tomorrow, unless there's something you need to get now."

He shook his head. "No, there's nothing I need."

"Just give me a minute, and we can go."

She managed to make it to the bathroom before the first sob hit her. She turned the water on to mask the sound, not wanting to humiliate herself any further. Dear heavens, she'd practically begged him to make love to her. And only hours after she'd thrown his declaration of love back in his face. Thank God the phone had rung and she'd spared herself that final mistake. Because getting any closer to Noah James would probably kill her. She lost her mind every time she was near him; she couldn't bear to lose her heart, too.

A quick scrub with a wet cloth washed away her ruined makeup, but there was nothing she could do about her red, swollen eyes. Or the dull ache in the center of her chest.

Noah was by the front door waiting for her when she came out. His eyes were hollow, his mouth grim. There was no sign of the fun-loving man she'd gotten to know over the past few days; this man was a hard wall of fear and regret.

Baby whined as she opened the door, sensing something wasn't right, or maybe just confused by the commotion at such a late hour. "I'll be back soon. Don't worry, everything is okay." She hoped she was telling the truth. Hadn't Noah said the baby wasn't his? Better not to ask, since her questions wouldn't change anything. The baby was coming, and it was coming now.

Outside the moon had settled near the horizon, but the stars were as bright as ever, little hard points of light in the summer sky. Night-blooming jasmine floated on a warm wind, its sweetness mocking the bitter ache in her throat.

They drove in silence, Noah furiously tapping on his phone screen, probably making flight arrangements. The highway was nearly deserted, her headlights lighting up the asphalt as they sped by mile after mile of grassland and scrub. Of course, the land was never truly empty, and she kept an eye out for wildlife. The last thing she needed was to hit bobcat or deer trying to cross the road.

Finally, she saw the exit for the airport and a minute later was merging onto the slightly busier road. Even at this time of night, Orlando had a decent amount of traffic, tractor trailers carrying goods to the countless outlet malls and shops, tour buses, and the intrepid citizens who worked the night shift.

"We're almost there. Did you get a flight?"

He didn't look at her, just kept staring out the window, the only sign of emotion the clenched fists in his lap. "Yeah, Southern Air. It leaves at five."

The glowing numbers on the dashboard clock showed it was almost three in the morning. He'd have plenty of time to check in and get through security. And plenty of time to worry. "Want me to go in with you? We could get some coffee or something while you wait."

"No."

So much for that idea. Not that she blamed him. He was worried about his child, and who knew what he was feeling towards his ex? She'd lied about her lies, and now the baby whose loss he'd mourned for was here in the flesh, waiting for him. He had a huge mess on his hands, and having to make small talk with the woman he'd nearly slept with only an hour ago certainly wasn't going to make his night any less complicated. Better to say goodbye quickly and let them both move on with their separate lives. Their holiday interlude had been magical, but reality was rearing its ugly head and no amount of wishing was going to change the facts. He had a baby, maybe even a family, if he could work things out with his ex. And she had a career just starting to take flight. If she could remember that, and not the way his mouth felt on hers, maybe she could say goodbye without embarrassing herself.

She pulled into the drop-off zone outside the terminal, leaving the engine running. He didn't even have any luggage to unload, nothing to slow him down or draw out the moment. Not that she was trying to stall him. The sooner he was out of the car, the sooner she could stop pretending everything was okay.

Noah unbuckled his seat belt, then looked to her, pain and longing warring in those soulful eyes. "Mollie... I'm sorry. I didn't mean for things to happen this way."

She forced a smile to her lips, feeling like her face

might crack from the unnatural expression. "Don't worry about me, I'm fine. Just go, be with your son. He needs you." She blinked, refusing to let her tears fall. "And Noah, if there's a possibility you and Angela can make things work, promise you'll try. You said you wanted to build relationships, and you have a second chance there if you want it."

He didn't answer, just brushed a stray lock of hair off her face and then let himself out of the car. And out of her life.

Noah had held on to the anger burning through him during the long, dark drive, using it to keep the fear and pain at bay. But looking into Mollie's eyes, bright with the tears she was trying so hard to hide, had been a torture that no amount of worry about the baby or hatred towards his ex could dull. He hadn't even been strong enough to say goodbye. Now she was gone, and he had to pull himself together.

He picked up his boarding pass, then took his turn in the security line, fighting to get back the numbness he'd perfected during all those goodbyes growing up. He'd learned as a child that there were situations in life you had no control over, and the only way to deal with them was to keep moving forward. But he'd never faced anything so terrifying before. What if the baby, his baby, wasn't okay? Angela's due date was weeks away—how early was too early? He should have asked the nurse when he'd had her on the phone. Hell, if Mollie hadn't been there to write down the name of the hospital, he might not even know where to go. His brain had short circuited the minute he'd heard the word *father*.

Of course, there was no guarantee he *was* the father. Angela could be lying again, for some ulterior motive only she understood. The nurse said there were paternity-test results, but how? He'd never been tested, although she could have stolen some hair from his brush or something. He wouldn't put that past her.

Still, he'd demand another test, one that he could make sure was on the up and up. But even paying for a DNA testing in a private lab would take a few days. What the heck did he do in the meantime? Could he trust anything Angela said? Could he let himself fall in love all over again with a baby that might not be his?

But deep inside, hadn't he always known it was his child? Wasn't that why he'd been so upset when Angela had run off? In his bones, he'd felt a bond with his unborn son, and whatever Angela had said in her note, he'd never stopped loving him.

Overwhelmed, he sank into a chair in front of his gate and automatically plugged in his phone to charge. At least that was productive. Desperate to keep his thoughts off of Angela and the baby, he flipped through some messages, but couldn't keep his mind on the words in front of him. Finally, he gave in and did what he'd been wanting to do since he got the phone call. He opened his wallet and pulled from its folds a black-and-white ultrasound photo. The technician had printed it for him months ago, pointing out the pixelated features of his son. He'd meant to throw it away after Angela's note, but hadn't been able to bring himself to actually do it. Or maybe he'd unconsciously held on to it out of hope, not wanting to believe the unborn baby he'd come to love belonged to another man.

Rubbing the wrinkled paper between his fingers, he realized it wasn't a matter of *if* he would be able to let down his guard and bond with the baby. The picture in his hand that he'd carried with him everywhere for the past four months showed it was too late for that. No, the real question was, how did he move forward from here?

"Is that your baby?" A middle-aged woman in a theme park T-shirt and too-tight yoga pants sat down next to him, her pink carry-on bag balanced on her lap.

Good question. Not knowing how to answer, he just nodded. Maybe she'd take a hint.

"Your first? I remember when I was expecting my first. We didn't have all those scans and tests and such back then. We had to wait until they were born to find out if it was a boy or a girl. Now, my daughter, she had a party when she found out with one of those cakes that you cut into—blue for a boy, pink for a girl. I think it's more fun to wait myself, but at least she knew what color to paint the nursery."

He nodded again and wondered how anyone could be so chipper before dawn.

"So, did you find out?"

"Excuse me?"

"The sex. Is it a boy or a girl? Or are you waiting to find out?"

"A boy." That he knew. It was everything else that he'd have to wait to find out about. If the baby was healthy. Why Angela had lied to him. He rubbed his eyes, suddenly exhausted.

"Are you okay?" The woman's eyes widened. "Oh my, is the baby... Is everything okay? I didn't even think—"

"I don't know." And the not knowing was killing him. "I got the call that my... The mother is in labor, but it's too soon. The due date isn't for another month." He wasn't sure why he was sharing all this with a stranger, maybe because saying it out loud made it more real. He needed to face the facts, and fast.

"Oh, how scary." The grandmotherly woman patted his hand reassuringly. "I'll say a prayer for him, but don't you worry. Doctors can do amazing things these days. A few weeks is nothing to worry about. Your son's going to be just fine, you'll see."

He nodded, swallowing past the lump in his throat. In his hands the grainy lines of the ultrasound blurred and his eyes stung. Damn it, he was not going to cry.

Thankfully, a bored-looking airline employee chose that moment to announce the boarding call for first class. "That's me." He gave a nod to his seatmate and stood.

"Good luck."

"Thanks." He needed all the luck he could get.

The ticket taker was efficient, if not personable, which was just fine with him. Soon he was settled in a window seat in a mostly empty section of the plane. It seemed midweek early-morning flights weren't popular with the first-class demographic. The half dozen other passengers sharing the space looked to be flying for business, whispering into phones or typing on their laptops right up until takeoff. Not a life he'd ever wanted to lead.

He'd worked part-time gigs over the years, made minimum wage doing various odd jobs, but he'd never felt tied to them. And now that he was actually making money as an artist, he could set his own hours, lead his own life. Not that he was doing very well in that regard. He was about to have a baby with one woman and had fallen head over heels with another. And he had no idea what he was supposed to do about any of it.

Chapter Six

Mollie woke to the sun shining in her eyes and a dog butt in her face. She vaguely remembered crashing on the couch when she got back from dropping Noah off. She should have gone to bed, but somehow being on the couch where they'd cuddled just hours before made him feel closer. Maybe that was pathetic, but Baby wasn't going to judge her. That was the great thing about dogs—they never made fun of you or told you to pull it together. Really, he'd just been excited to be allowed on the couch at all. She normally had a firm rule against dogs on the furniture, but she'd also had a firm rule against falling in love. Rules weren't her thing, obviously.

"Go on, move over." Baby grudgingly moved an inch, probably afraid he was about to lose his coveted spot. "Fine, stay there. But I'm getting up."

She left the big dog sprawled across the cushions while she used the bathroom and brushed her teeth. She avoided the mirror entirely. No good could come of that, not after three hours of sleep and another two of crying. Instead, she finger-combed her hair by feel and pulled on her comfiest sweats. Today was her last day of vacation; maybe a walk on the beach would put things in perspective. That, and a cup of coffee.

She gathered her camera bag and the dog's leash while her old-fashioned percolator heated, filling the air with the world's best aroma. Maybe if she took deep enough breaths she could absorb some of the caffeine while she waited for it to finish. Finally it stopped bubbling and she poured the dark, rich coffee into a thermos with milk and sugar. "Come on, Baby. You can't stay on the couch forever."

The big dog blinked slowly as if considering doing exactly that, before finally clambering down, one leg at a time. She let him do his business outside, then loaded him into the car for the short drive to the Sandpiper. Paradise had a public beach, but she'd gotten in the habit of parking in the Sandpiper's lot and starting from that end. Probably because that way she could raid the big commercial refrigerators before going home. Her own food stash tended towards stale crackers and outdated yogurt more often than not.

She parked at the far end of the lot and skirted the inn itself, sticking to the sandy path that wove through the grounds and down to the beach. Jillian should be at work on a Friday morning, but she wasn't taking any chances. Sympathy from her friend would just send her over the edge. She needed clarity, not company.

The beach itself was nearly deserted, just a few retired fishermen surf casting, unable to stay away from the water where they'd spent the better part of their lives.

She returned their waves as she and Baby walked by, taking comfort in the normalcy of the moment. Her life might feel like it was spinning on its axis, but no matter what, there would always be old men fishing on the beach, as constant as the tides themselves.

She strolled right at the water's edge, where the wet sand was hard-packed and easier to walk on. Baby kept pace, eyeing the chattering gulls but not giving chase. He was a constant, too; she could count on him even when doubting herself. They walked for about a mile, passing the most deserted part of the shore before hitting the public beach area. Ahead, she spotted a young boy tossing a ball and she tightened her grip on the leash.

"Not yours, Baby." The dog had an addiction to fetch, despite his missing limb, and was liable to beg, borrow or steal any ball he came across. He whined pathetically but didn't attempt to pull away.

"Hi! Can I pet your dog?" The freckle-faced child smiled up at her, no fear showing despite the fact the dog probably outweighed him three times over.

Baby whined again and nudged the ball in the boy's hand.

"Sure, if your mom says it's okay."

"Mo-om! Can I pet the dog? The lady said I had to ask you first."

Mollie grinned as a woman around her own age got up from her beach chair, shaking her head at her son's exuberance. "Hi, I'm Gina. This guy," she ruffled his hair affectionately, "is Benji. I hope he wasn't bothering you. He just really loves animals."

"I'm Mollie, and no, he's fine. Baby loves to make new friends. And he especially loves kids."

"Baby?" She smiled. "I guess that's better than Tiny."

Mollie chuckled. "It's probably good I didn't think of that, or I might have gone with it."

"So, can I, Mom? Please?"

"Sure." To Mollie, she whispered, "He's been wanting a dog for ages, I'm thinking maybe for Christmas. I'll have finished the manuscript I'm working on by then, so I'll have more time to spend training a puppy."

"Good plan. You don't want to get into a position where you're overwhelmed."

Gina laughed, her eyes dancing. "I think that ship has sailed. Being a stay-at-home mom while trying to have a writing career is more than I bargained for. Not that I'd change a thing."

"That does sound tough. What kind of writing do you do?"

"I write mystery novels. As much as I love being home with him, I think it will be a lot easier once he starts kindergarten. Until then, it's…interesting. Yesterday I was in the middle of this gory murder scene and had to stop midsentence to help him use the potty." She shook her head, grinning. "I thought about putting off writing until he's older, but I'd be lost without it, you know? It's just part of who I am."

"How do you manage it?" There she went, blurting out whatever she was thinking. It wasn't any of her business how this woman managed her time. But she talked about writing the same way Mollie felt about her photography. It was a part of her identity, and she couldn't imagine giving it up.

The young mother shrugged and watched her son. "I have a great babysitter, and I get a lot done during his naps. Then when my husband gets home in the evening, he handles the bath and bedtime so I can squeeze in some more hours then." She stroked the dog's fur as she thought. "It's hard sometimes, and I don't get anywhere near as much sleep as I'd like, but it's totally worth it."

Mollie nodded, trying to fit this woman's experience into the mental dividers in her head. Wife, mother, writer. Of course she'd known in theory that plenty of women worked and had families. Cassie certainly managed, but Mollie had somehow drawn a mental line between a scheduled workweek and more creative pursuits. An artist's muse didn't follow a set schedule and she'd assumed someone like Gina would end up secretly resentful of the time she lost to her family. "No regrets, huh?"

Gina grinned at her son, who was now covered in dog slobber and sand. "Never. But speaking of getting it all done, I've got to take him home for his nap. Thanks for letting him make friends with Baby."

"Anytime." Mollie watched the pair leave and then headed farther down the beach. She had a lot to think about and plenty of ground to cover while she did it.

* * *

Back in Atlanta, Noah's car was waiting for him in long-term parking, a tiny piece of normalcy in a world that no longer felt like his. The traffic was also normal, which meant it had been nearly an hour and he still wasn't at the hospital. An hour that seemed like forever, on top of the lifetime he'd already spent on the plane. He'd tried to nap in the air, but despite his exhaustion he couldn't stop his thoughts long enough to fall asleep. His brain was a constantly turning carousel, rotating between his anger at Angela, his worry for his son and his heartbreak at leaving Mollie. If he'd had a little more time with her, maybe he could have gained her trust, convinced her that he would never stand in the way of who she wanted to be. As it was, he'd groped her and then run out, flying hundreds of miles away to see another woman give birth to his child. Not the way to convince Mollie he was serious about her. No, he'd marked himself as a drama magnet, and no doubt she was glad to be rid of him.

Finally he spotted the sign for St. Luke's. He wove through the lot, eventually spotting a car pulling out. He snagged the spot, then jogged into the towering steel and glass building. Moving felt good, a way to take some action and burn off the adrenaline souring his stomach. Inside, the icy air hit him like a fist, slamming him with the scents of disinfectant and disease. Damn it, he hated hospitals. Anything medical, really. But none of this was about his likes or dislikes, so he forced what he hoped was a pleasant look on his face and asked the volunteer at the reception desk where to find Angela.

"Third floor, in the west tower." It sounded like the kind of directions you'd get in a medieval castle. But he dutifully took the paper visitor's badge and stuck it to his shirt before heading to the bank of elevators she'd indicated. He passed an enormous fish tank and briefly wondered why it was that all hospitals seemed to have fish. Maybe unconsciously the designers recognized that the fish were trapped just like the patients were, in tightly controlled environments calibrated to their specific needs. A depressing thought, probably not what the hospital had in mind when it added the tank.

On the third floor, he found himself in a yet another lobby, a smaller one with framed pictures of teddy bears on the walls. A frosted glass window led to what he assumed was the labor and delivery area. He rang the bell and a nurse slid the window open. "Can I help you?"

"I'm here to see Angela Garner. Someone called me and told me she was in labor."

"Are you a relative?"

He swallowed hard. "I'm the baby's father."

She nodded and typed something into the keyboard in front of her. "The doctor is checking her now. When he's done, I'll have someone come and get you. It shouldn't be too long."

"Thank you." He flopped down in one of the chairs and absently grabbed a magazine. *The Illustrated Guide to Breastfeeding.* No, just no. He tossed it down and rested his head in his hands.

Minutes passed. An older couple came in, the wife

in tears, the husband beaming, his chest stuck out like prize rooster. *I'm the Grandpa* was emblazoned on his shirt in big black letters. Crap, Noah hadn't called his parents. He'd do so later, when he knew what was going on.

The nurse at the desk buzzed the proud grandparents through and then answered the phone. A frown crossed her face for just a second before her features smoothed into a more neutral expression. Speaking softly, she watched Noah, and he felt a premonition come over him. He watched her hang up, unable to move.

"Mr. James, I'm afraid there have been some complications."

Complications? What the hell did that mean?

"The baby isn't tolerating labor, so they're taking Ms. Garner in for surgery. She's on her way to the operating room now."

"Operating room?" A ball of fear solidified in his stomach, settling like lead on the ocean floor. "What? How?" He didn't even know what to ask. Had no idea what to do. He'd been signed up to take a weekend childbirth course, but Angela had left him before it had started.

"She's having a cesarean section. The baby's in distress, so they need to act fast. She'll be under general anesthesia, so I'm afraid you can't go back with her. But if you have a seat, I'll let you know when she's out of surgery."

Holy hell, distress? What did that even mean? "Just tell me, is she going to be okay? Is the baby okay?"

The nurse's eyes softened briefly. "I'll try to get an update for you as soon as I can. All right?"

"Yeah, I guess it has to be." He somehow made it over to one of the chairs lining the wall, then popped up again, unable to stay in one place. Pacing the ridiculously decorated room, he realized just how over his head he was. He needed backup. Instantly, his mind went to Mollie, but that was hardly a viable option. No, there was only one person he could call right now and know they'd pick up.

Taking out his phone, he dialed the number by heart. As he expected, it was answered on the first ring. "Hey, Dad. It's Noah."

Mollie walked on the beach for another hour, the young mother's words stuck in her head. No regrets. Wasn't that what she wanted, a life with no regrets? She'd vowed to stay single and pursue her career because she didn't want to look back and wonder, "What if?" But Gina's words offered a whole other perspective. Mollie had been so focused on her photography she hadn't thought about how many other things she might lose out on. Somehow she'd assumed that a relationship, a family, would all be there when she was ready for them, if she ever was. Like she could schedule a lover the way she scheduled her twice-a-year dentist visits. What if she missed her chance at love, and it wasn't waiting for her when she was ready for it? What if there was a whole other world of regret she'd never really considered? Was she making the same mistake her mother had, closing off one part of herself to fulfill another? At least her mother had her scrapbooks and those old programs—Mollie just had that single photo of Noah she'd snapped on the boat. Would that be enough to satisfy her if she ended up alone in her old age?

Feeling more lost than when she'd woken up this morning, she let her steps take her up into the old inn. Jillian wasn't there, but she could at least get some more coffee and a muffin and hope the sugar and caffeine would kick-start her brain. Murphy greeted them eagerly, barking and bouncing around Baby, but the bigger, older dog was too worn out from their walk to do much more than wag his tail in return. "Sorry, Murphy. We should have taken you with us, I wasn't thinking. Next time you can go, too."

"Go where?"

Mollie turned at the sound of Nic's voice, nearly tripping over Baby, who had collapsed in a heap in the middle of the floor. "The beach. I took Baby for a long walk and now he's too tuckered out to play. If I'd been thinking, I would have stopped and picked up Murphy on my way."

"Don't let him fool you. I already took him for a jog first thing this morning. He ran three miles, and if he had any sense at all he would be snoozing like Baby. He's just too rock-headed to know he's tired."

Mollie ruffled the border collie's ears, smiling at his goofy dog grin. "Don't you listen to him, boy. He's just jealous that you're in better shape than he is."

Nic laughed and stepped around her to the big coffeepot they kept constantly filled for their guests. "Want some?"

"Do you even have to ask?" He handed her a steaming mug and she helped herself to the cream and sugar. "I don't suppose you have any muffins left over from breakfast?"

"In the bread box."

She grabbed a blueberry one and bit down into pure, sugar-filled decadence. "Yum. I needed that, thanks."

He waved off the appreciation and leaned against the counter, sipping his own coffee. "So, you want to talk about it?"

She swallowed, the sweet muffin turning to sawdust in her mouth. "Talk about what?"

"Noah leaving, finding out he's going to be a father. Or the weather, your pick."

How did Nic know about any of that?

Seeing the question on her face, he grinned. "Don't worry, I'm not a mind reader. Noah texted me from the airport, asking me to ship his luggage to his place in Atlanta. Naturally I asked if everything was all right, and he explained about the baby."

She tried to force a smile but gave up. "Yeah, it sucks."

"Sounds like it. So, what are you going to do?"

"Do? There's nothing left for me to do. He's gone. He needs to figure out his life, and I'm moving on with mine. End of story."

"Uh-huh." Nic looked less than convinced. "So that's it?"

"Why wouldn't it be? He was only here on vacation. For heaven's sake, he was supposed to be on his honeymoon with another woman. We had some fun, but it was never supposed to be anything more than that."

"So you're not in love with him, then?"

"No."

Nic raised an eyebrow.

"Fine, maybe." She clenched the coffee mug like a lifeline. "But that doesn't matter. He needs to focus on his family now, not me. Who knows, maybe he and his ex will get back together now that he knows it's his baby."

Nic rolled his eyes. "Right, because nothing makes a guy want to give a girl a second chance like finding out she lied to him. Noah is not that stupid."

He had a point. "Even still, he has a kid now. That's got to be his priority."

"And having a child means you can't have a relationship? I'll make sure to tell Jillian we need to get divorced once the baby comes."

"Not the same thing. You were together before you started a family."

"Okay, then how about Cassie and Alex? Should they not have gotten married just because she already had a child? Would that have been best for Emma?"

She opened her mouth then closed it. Emma adored her stepfather and was blossoming with all the extra attention that her new grandmother and aunt gave her. And Cassie had never been so happy. "You're a pain in the butt. Don't you have guests to greet or something?"

"Not right now. And someone has to talk some sense into you. Jillian's at work, so you get me." He softened his voice and gave a wry smile. "Trust me, I've been there. When I met Jillian, I told myself there were a million reasons it couldn't work. But it did. Love is always a risk, but it's one worth taking."

"Wow. I didn't know you were such a romantic. Did you steal that off a greeting card or something?"

"Probably. But it's still true. At least consider it, okay?"

"I'll think about it." She couldn't stop thinking about Noah. But that about him wasn't going to change anything. No matter how much she wanted it to.

Chapter Seven

Noah had known his father would come. A man of few words, his dad had simply asked which floor to go to and then hung up. That his mother had come with him was more of a surprise, although maybe it shouldn't have been. Didn't all women get worked up over the idea of grandchildren? Still, his parents usually managed to avoid being in the same room together. They had a tendency to combust when kept in close quarters and Noah felt the tension flooding his system ratchet up a few degrees.

"Have you heard anything?" His mom gave him a hard hug, then stroked his face the way she had when he was a kid.

He shook his head. It had been half an hour since

they'd told him Angela was being taken to surgery. "I'm hoping no news is good news."

"That's exactly right." His father patted him on the shoulder. "These things take time. I can't tell you how long I waited for news when your mother was having you. I was getting ready to punch my way back there when they finally told me you were both okay."

Noah's felt the muscles in his neck relax an infinitesimal amount. "Yeah, the idea did cross my mind."

His mom took his arm and led him to a chair. "Sit, tell us what happened. I thought she'd taken off, that she said you weren't the father."

"That what I thought, too. But when the hospital called, they made it clear that she's saying I am. They took her back to surgery before I could see her, so I didn't get a chance to ask her why she lied or what kind of game she's trying to play now."

His father nodded thoughtfully. "You'll have testing done, I suppose."

"She already did, or so she says."

"And you believe her?"

He shrugged. "I probably shouldn't, but yeah, I do. I'll pay for another test, to be certain, but my gut tells me she's telling the truth this time. So I'm here."

"Of course you are. You're not the kind of person that could turn your back on a woman and child in need, no matter what the circumstances." His mother's confidence in him helped ease the sting of Angela's betrayal.

"I just feel like an idiot."

His father's head snapped up. "Don't even go there. You took her at her word, you stood by her when she said it was yours and you did what you could to track her down even after she left you. Your actions have been honorable. That hers haven't is no reflection on you or that baby."

Humbled, he nodded. He had done the best he could and would have to figure out the rest as he came to it. He started to say "thank you," then spotted someone in scrubs out of the corner of his eye.

"Noah James?"

"Yes." He stood, wanting to take whatever news she had for him on his feet, like a man.

"Your girlfriend is in recovery. She's going to be out of it for quite some time. But I can take you to the NICU to see your son if you'd like."

The breath he'd been holding whooshed out of him all at once. "Are they okay?"

She smiled. "They're both stable. Your son gave us a scare in labor, but his APGAR scores were good and he's breathing on his own. They took him to the NICU more as a precaution than anything else."

"What kind of scores?"

"APGAR scores are a way to judge how well a baby is doing in the first few minutes of life. He passed with top marks."

"And I can see him? Now?"

"Just follow me. Oh, and you're allowed two people at a time in the NICU, so if you want to bring someone back with you…"

He turned back to his parents. "Mom? Want to come?"

She sniffed and wiped a tear from the corner of her eye. "Wild horses couldn't keep me away."

"Dad, you okay out here?"

"I'm fine. Your mother would have me court mar-
tialed if I tried to cut in line ahead of her. I'll go find
us some coffee or something. You two take your time."

"This way, please." The nurse used her badge to open
the heavy automatic doors, leading them through a laby-
rinth of hallways. Finally they stopped in an alcove next
to a glassed-in room. The nurse pointed to a large sink.
"First you need to wash your hands up the elbows, re-
moving any rings or bracelets. Then I'll give you each
a gown to put on over your clothes."

This whole thing was surreal. He scrubbed as thoroughly as he could, but all he could think was that this
was it. He was going to meet his son.

He probably should hold something back, just in case
this was all an elaborate plot concocted by Angela. Gut
feeling or not. But when they were finally gowned up
and ushered into the nursery, he knew it was a losing
battle. He let the nurse squirt sanitizing gel into his already clean hands, his heart thumping triple time in
his chest. There was no way he could hold back or be
logical about this. "Mr. James, this little guy would
like to meet you."

The nurse beckoned him over to some kind of space-
age plastic crib, with more lights and monitors than he'd
imagined could fit in such a small space. His mother
took his hand, squeezing tightly when she looked at the
tiny baby inside. "Oh, Noah, he's the spitting image of
you as a newborn."

The little one had pale skin that looked a size too big
for him, but he was awake and alert, watching them as

intently as they watched him. The full head of curly hair looked a bit out of place on such a young baby, but what had Noah's breath catching in his chest were his eyes. They were the same ones he saw looking back at him from the mirror every day, the eyes he'd gotten from his father and his grandfather before that. "He's really mine. He's my son."

"Can I hold him, please?" The nurse checked the chart once, then adjusted the wire that led from the beeping machine beside her to a small, heart-shaped sticker on the baby's chest. "He's all yours, Daddy."

Noah slid one hand under the baby's head, relishing the feel of his soft curls, and the other under the diaper-clad bottom. "Like this?"

"That's it."

Trembling with awe, he lifted the baby boy to his chest and felt the hot tears he had been holding back slide down his face. His son. Whatever else happened, he was a father now. And he was going to do whatever it took to stay in his son's life, no matter what Angela tried to pull.

Noah spent the rest of the day just holding his son, letting go only so that his parents could take their turns. He'd even gotten to feed the little guy his first bottle. But now it was time for the seven o'clock shift change and the nurses were about to kick him out.

"Go get dinner or visit your girlfriend. She should be on the postpartum floor by now."

Noah didn't bother to correct the assumption, feeling a pang of guilt for not having thought of Angela earlier. He might never forgive her for her lies, but she was the mother of his child and he could have at least checked on her. "Has she been asking to see the baby?"

The pretty nurse colored, her cheeks flushing as she averted her eyes. "Um, not that I've heard. But surgery can be rough. I'm sure she'll be asking to visit tomorrow, once she's feeling a bit stronger."

Understanding hit him. It wasn't that Angela was unable to visit the baby. She just didn't want to. Which made an awful kind of sense, as much as he hated to admit it. Maybe she was just tired, like the nurse said, but Angela had a bad habit of avoiding anything she thought might be difficult. If that was the case, well, she was going to have to grow up—whether she liked it or not. Starting right now.

He'd wanted to rush right up to Angela's room, but his parents had insisted on getting dinner together before they left. He'd chewed through a soggy tuna sandwich without tasting anything other than his own impatience and was now nursing a cup of lukewarm coffee while his parents shared a piece of chocolate cake.

"Don't make assumptions, son." His father stared him down, apparently picking up on Noah's ill-concealed anger. "She just gave birth, and she had a pretty bad time of it from the sounds of things. You don't know what she's thinking or why she hasn't seen the baby yet."

"Right." It was true he had no idea what she was thinking, but then he obviously never really had. And what's more, he didn't care. All he needed to know was that she was going to do the right thing by the baby and by him. Once he'd talked to her, they could work everything else out through their lawyers. Her daddy's old money would certainly pay for hers and he'd had one on retainer since she walked out on him.

"Your father's right, of course. She may just be having a hard time of it. But I'm willing to say now that I never trusted her. Don't go up there and attack the woman, but be on your guard. I wouldn't put anything past her, not after what she did. The thought of her keeping a son from his father..." She shook her head, her stylishly bobbed and highlighted hair shimmering even under the cheap hospital lighting. "Just don't let her suck you back in. Just because you love your son doesn't mean you have to be with his mother. No good can come of that kind of a marriage."

"One like yours, you mean?" Crap, where did that come from?

"Excuse me?" His mother arched one perfectly arched eyebrow. "What's wrong with my relationship with your father?"

Noah looked from one parent to the other, desperately wishing he'd kept his damn mouth shut. Either the lack of sleep or the shock of fatherhood seemed to have broken the part of his brain that filtered his thoughts before he said them. Crumpling his napkin, he tried to backtrack. "Nothing. I just know you two tend to be... volatile." And argumentative, and stubborn, and sometimes even a tiny bit manipulative.

His mother's eyes widened in surprise before she burst out laughing. She thought it was funny? Were all women crazy?

His father reached over and pecked her on the cheek

before turning back to Noah, an easy grin on his face. "Your mom and I fight, but it doesn't mean anything."

Huh? "So it's some kind of game for you?"

"I wouldn't say that," his mother interjected. "Your father and I just have very different views on a lot of things. And we're a bit hardheaded about it. But we never take offense, right, honey?"

"Right. I'd hate to have a pushover for a wife. Your mother keeps me on my toes, battle-ready so to speak. If it wasn't for her, I might have gone soft in my old age. She challenges me, and I like that."

He blinked, his synapses short-circuiting. "Wait, you like fighting with each other?"

His mom shrugged. "I wouldn't call it fighting. We just both like to express our opinions."

Right. Whatever. If constantly disagreeing made his parents happy, well, then, he was happy for them. But it was still crazy, and not what he wanted in a relationship. He wanted someone who had his back and understood him even when he didn't understand himself. He wanted Mollie.

He stood up from the table, shoving any thoughts of Mollie to the back of his mind. He couldn't deal with that right now. But he could go handle whatever drama Angela had cooked up. And by then the NICU visiting hours would have started up again and he could spend the night with his son. "Thanks for the dinner, and thanks for coming. It meant a lot."

"Of course we came. And we'll be back tomorrow, to check on you and visit our grandbaby. Like it or not, you aren't going to be able to keep us away."

A few months ago, the thought of more family time with his parents would have been terrifying, but not tonight. "Good. Now go home. I'll see you tomorrow."

He somehow found his way back to that original waiting room with the stuffed bear pictures on the wall. This time he spoke with more confidence when the nurse at the window asked him his name. "Noah James, here to visit Angela Garner."

The woman buzzed him back, then directed him down a long hallway in the same direction as the NICU. "Postpartum rooms are in that wing. She's in 1102."

He hadn't realized how near she'd been before. Probably better that way. He was still upset, but his parents had been right; some food and a mental break had left him feeling slightly more in control. But just slightly.

At the very end of the hallway, he found room 1102. The door was partially opened, but he knocked anyway.

"Come in."

He eased the door open and walked in, then stopped at the foot of the bed. He didn't know what he'd expected to find, but it wasn't this. Angela was wearing an embroidered robe and silk nightgown, the teal color picking up the green in her eyes. Her heavily made-up eyes. She was in full makeup and her hair was perfectly arranged. But more surprising than that was the random guy sitting at her bedside.

"Noah, you came!" Angela's surprise sounded real. Had she really thought he'd ignore her call?

"They said you were in labor, that the baby was mine."

"Well, of course it's yours, silly."

He fisted his hands in his pants pockets. "You said in your letter that you'd lied, that he wasn't."

"Oh, that. I was just upset. You didn't really believe me, did you?"

"I didn't know what to believe. Or where you were. Or if my baby, if it was my baby, was okay. But mostly, yeah, I believed you because what else could I do? You left, Angela."

Her face contorted into her version of a frown, one that was careful not to cause any wrinkles. "I was hormonal. And you weren't treating me well." She reached over and patted Mr. Polo-and-Khakis on the hand. Who at least had the good grace to look uncomfortable about the whole situation.

"If by treating you well, you mean letting you spend all my money on whatever you wanted, I guess I didn't. But this is a life you're talking about. Not a disagreement over what movie to watch."

"Fine, you're right. I thought you might get like this. That's why I had the paternity test done. All they needed was your toothbrush. Crazy what they can do these days."

Damn, his toothbrush. He'd noticed it was missing, but had assumed the cleaning lady had tossed it. That Angela would have swiped it had never occurred to him.

"So are we okay now?"

Nothing about what she'd done was okay, but there was no point in pressing her. Changing the subject, he gestured to the third party in the room. "Going to introduce me to your friend?"

Angela flashed a brilliant smile, and he remembered

why he'd initially fallen for her. Or rather, been sucked in by her. She was gorgeous on the outside. It was the inside that was the problem. "Oh, yes, Noah, this is Dick. He was nice enough to let me stay with him while I was sorting things out."

Noah just barely managed to stifle a laugh. She'd left him for a guy named Dick? Speaking of names— "The hospital wanted to know if we had a name for him."

Angela's nose crunched in confusion. "For who?"

Noah counted to ten and reminded himself she was probably on a lot of painkillers. "The baby. They want to know what we are naming the baby."

"Oh. Well, I thought you'd want to name him, since it's a boy. All the fun names are girl names."

All right, then. "How about Ryan after my father?"

She nodded absently. "That's fine. Can you come up with a middle name, too? And tell the nurses?"

Yeah, he could do that. "Do you want me to see about taking you down there to visit him? I'm pretty sure I can commandeer a wheelchair if you need one."

She looked at her new boy toy, then back to him. "I don't think so… I'm so tired. And I've got a visitor, I wouldn't want to be rude and leave him all alone while I went traipsing around the hospital."

Noah's jaw dropped. Surely she didn't mean what she was saying. "You don't want to go see your baby, whom you haven't seen yet, because you're entertaining?"

"I said I was tired, too. And sore. You have no idea how hard this all was on me. Besides, I wouldn't even know what to do. I'm sure I'd just be in the way."

He kept his temper in check—she *had* just had major

surgery, and who knows how many hours of labor before that? Maybe she just needed some time to rest. But very soon they were going to have a serious talk. Alone.

Mollie had spent the afternoon at her computer, editing images, looking for ones good enough to include in the upcoming show. Tedious but creative, the work was detailed enough to keep her mind off of Noah, at least mostly. At nine, she finally finished. Wincing a bit, she stretched her kinked-up muscles and realized she was starving. She'd somehow forgotten both lunch and dinner. She'd made real progress, though, so a grumbling tummy wasn't too high a price to pay.

"How about you? You hungry, too?" Baby thumped his tail in response. "Okay, then, let's get some dinner." She padded into the kitchen and filled Baby's bowl with kibble, then added half a can of wet food as a treat. She poured herself a bowl of chocolate-frosted cereal and milk, and then carried it to the tiny kitchen table to eat. Her phone was there where she'd thrown it when she'd come home, the message light blinking. Oops. She picked it up, and saw she had three text messages. One was from Jillian, asking how she was. She texted back, Okay. Call you tomorrow, and thumbed down to the next.

The next two were from Noah.

The first read: Sorry about everything.

The next was a picture of a newborn, with the words: He's okay.

She thumbed back, So glad with shaking hands. Looking at the photo, there was no question the baby was his. It looked like a tiny, slightly wrinkled version of Noah. Which meant he really was a father now. Was he happy? Scared? Was he angry at Angela, or had he looked past her mistakes for the sake of his son?

Mollie set the phone down and stared at it. What was she supposed to do now? Call him? Pretend she'd never met him? Drown her feelings in sugary cereal?

The phone rang, vibrating on the table. It was Noah. Taking a deep breath, she picked it up.

"Hi, Noah."

"Hey." He sounded good. Tired, but good. "I hope it's okay to call. I saw you had texted back, and I figured I'd take a chance."

"Of course you can call. I'm happy to hear everything is all right."

"Yeah, he's great. His name's Ryan Thomas. He's five pounds, nine ounces and healthy. They're saying he should be able to move to the regular nursery tomorrow, as long as he keeps doing well overnight."

The pride in his voice had her blinking back tears. "I'm sure he will do well. He's a lucky little boy. And Angela, is she okay, too?"

"Um, yeah. Better than expected, in fact. We still need to sit down and talk about everything, though."

She fought to keep the jealousy out of her voice. "That's great. Well, I should let you get back to them, and I've got a ton of work to do before the gallery show. Have a good night."

"You, too. And Mollie, I really am sorry. About everything."

"Yeah, me, too. Goodbye, Noah."

She stared at the phone for another few minutes after hanging up. He was happy; that's what should matter. And it did matter. It just also sucked to know that he was happy there, with his ex and his baby, snuggling and bonding, while she was here eating soggy cereal with her dog.

Worse, she wasn't just jealous because he was with his ex. No, she was actually jealous that Angela was the one with the baby. With Noah's baby. Which was just plain stupid. She'd never felt her biological clock so much as tick, and now, looking at the baby picture on her phone, it was in full alarm mode.

Just the thought of a child should terrify her, even if it was Noah's baby. Especially if it was Noah's baby. Man, love really did mess with your head.

Thankfully, she had the upcoming show to distract herself with, not to mention the summer semester starting on Monday. She had plenty to keep her busy and keep her away from Noah. Maybe in a while she would consider the idea of a relationship, a family, but not right now. Not with Noah. He deserved a chance to figure things out on his own without worrying about her. More to the point, his son deserved all of his father's attention right now. Learning to parent a newborn and hashing things out with the ex would be hard enough without adding a long-distance relationship to the mix. If she cared about him at all she'd let him navigate his new life without any extra encumbrances or demands. And she did care, more than she wanted to. Which meant there was only one thing to do.

She picked up her phone and looked at the picture

one more time before hitting delete. Then, her stomach clenching, she forced herself to block his number. They needed a clean break. If he kept calling her, she'd eventually cave and tell him how she felt, and she was not going to pressure him like that. This was the right thing to do, for both of them.

But man, it felt awful. Sliding out of her chair she sat down on the kitchen floor and wrapped her arms around her dog. Thank God dogs didn't have drama. She couldn't handle any more.

Chapter Eight

Noah hefted the car seat carrying his sleeping son in one hand and knocked as softly as he could on the apartment door with the other. No way was he risking the doorbell—Ryan had just fallen asleep and he'd rather face a lion unarmed than an overtired baby. He could hear muted noises on the other side of the door, but after several long minutes and repeated knocks, no one answered. Angela knew he was coming by now with the baby. Noah had been keeping him at his apartment ever since he'd been discharged so that Angela could rest and recover from the C-section. But it had been over a week, and they were supposed to switch off. He'd even paid for a nanny so she'd have help with Ryan.

Maybe that's who he could hear inside, and Angela had gone out for something? If the nanny had just started, she might not feel comfortable answering the door. Either way, he wasn't going to keep standing outside when he had a perfectly good key in his pocket. He let himself in and spotted Angela's favorite designer purse sitting on the entryway table with her keys. So she *was* here. Maybe he'd just knocked too softly for her to hear him. He passed through into the large living room, his steps muffled by the plush wall-to-wall carpeting. Seeing no sign of anyone, he set the car seat, sleeping baby and all, on the floor and headed down the hall towards the back of the apartment.

Angela's bedroom door was open, and he could see her standing in front of the bed with her back to him. "Hey," he called out. "Sorry to barge in, but I was trying to be quiet so I didn't wake the baby."

Startled, she spun around, clutching a folded sweater to her chest. Was she doing laundry? That didn't sound like her; she sent all her clothes out to be cleaned. "Noah, I didn't think you'd be here so early."

"I said after lunch. It's one o'clock."

She darted a nervous glance at the clock on the nightstand. "Oh, I must have lost track of time." Her face was pinched, as if he'd interrupted something and she wished he'd go. Looking around, he realized the normally tidy room was a mess, with clothes thrown on every surface. Two suitcases with trendy logos on them were on the floor beside her, a smaller one on the bed. A sick, dark pain curled deep in his chest.

"What the hell's going on here?"

She smiled just a shade too brightly. He knew her

manipulative ways too well to fall for that. "I'm just…
going through my things."

"That's bull and you know it. You're packing. Why?
Where are you going this time?" He heard the baby fuss
outside and panic took over. "If you were planning to
take my son away from me, you'll have to do it over my
dead body. It's time to grow up, Angela. It's not about
you and your temper tantrums anymore. We've got a
kid, and he deserves to grow up in a stable family. That
means we have to try to get along, no matter how we
feel about each other. No running off, and no more lies.
He deserves better than your petty schemes."

Her eyes filled, and for once he thought maybe, just
maybe, he was seeing the real Angela, not the facade
she normally wore. "Don't you think I know that?"
She dropped the sweater onto the bed, and wiped her
eyes, smearing her makeup. "I know I'm flighty and
irresponsible. Maybe it's genetic. My mom certainly
never won a Mother of the Year award. And I'm definitely not anywhere near ready to settle down and be
the kind of person that has a kid. I mean, look at me.
Do I look like someone's mom?"

What she looked like was a confused and spoiled girl
trying to play dress-up. He almost felt sorry for her, but
the baby in the next room was the one that deserved his
compassion. Angela had used up her share long ago. "It
doesn't matter what you look like. The fact is, you have
a child, and you need to start acting like it."

"No, actually I don't."

"What the hell does that mean?" He was too tired to
play games, and Ryan's cries were getting more urgent.

Stalking back down the hall, he went to the kitchen to make up a fresh bottle of formula. And found nothing there but wine and leftovers from the high-end restaurant down the street. Where was all the baby stuff? "Where's the formula? He's due for a bottle, and now is as good a time as any to show you how to mix it up."

"I don't have any. Didn't you bring some?"

He counted to ten silently before answering. "No, I didn't bring some, because I assumed that you would have the basics, like formula and bottles and diapers. But I guess I overestimated you. Again." He shoved a hand through his hair. He needed this to work, and getting angry wasn't going to fix things. "I'll run down to the store. We can finish talking when I get back."

"No." She stood in the kitchen doorway, blocking him in.

"Angela, whatever is going on, we'll work it out when I get back, okay? I'm sorry I yelled, but damn it, this is exactly the kind of thing I'm talking about."

"I didn't buy that stuff because I didn't plan for him to be here."

"Angela, I know the pregnancy was a surprise, but you've had nine freaking months to get used to the idea. That's more than enough time to stock up on some bottles. Hell, you don't even have to fill them. That's what the nanny is for."

She looked down, avoiding his eyes. "She's not coming. I fired her. And before you ask why, it's because I'm not going to need a nanny."

He rolled his eyes. "Please, you don't even have the

basic necessities, and you've never changed a diaper in your life."

"That's right, and I don't intend to start." She shrugged, and her eyes clouded a bit. "We both know I wouldn't be any good at it anyway."

What was she saying? "You'll learn. Everyone has to learn."

"I don't. I'm leaving. Dick's flying me to New York City. He has an apartment on the Upper East Side."

Was her boyfriend's yuppie address supposed to impress him? "I don't care if he lives in the top of the Empire State Building. You can't just come and go whenever you feel like it and dump Ryan off on me like you're taking a dog to the kennel." Man, he should have expected this. Too tired to argue, he headed back to the living room to get Ryan. "Fine. When are you getting back? We can work out a custody schedule then."

"That's what I'm trying to tell you. I'm not coming back, and I don't want custody."

Noah stopped, his legs frozen to the floor. "You don't mean that."

"Oh, I do. I mean, he's a cute baby and everything, but I'm just not cut out for motherhood. And Dick, he needs me up in New York right now."

"And your son doesn't need you?" Rage fought with denial. "You're what? Just going to give him to me and pretend this never happened?"

"If I can." She blinked back a few more tears. "In fact, it's probably best we don't stay in contact—no use picking at old wounds and all."

Grabbing the baby carrier, he stalked for the door. "Don't worry. The only contact you'll have from now on is with my lawyer."

Mollie eyed her suitcase and the black spiked heels sitting beside it. She'd packed and repacked for Atlanta three times, but she couldn't make it all fit. Normally she was a minimalist, but she had no idea what she was going to feel like wearing, and in a fit of desperation had shoved what seemed like every outfit she owned into her only piece of luggage. Which would be fine if she could just get it closed. With her shoes in it.

The sound of the doorbell broke her standoff with the recalcitrant suitcase. "Come in, Mom. I'm back here." Baby scurried to the front door to act as greeter, leaving on her own.

"Aren't you ready? We need to get going."

Like she didn't already know that. "I'm almost done. I'm just packing a few last things."

Her mom walked into the room and then stopped, her jaw dropping open at the tangled mess of clothes spilling out of the suitcase. "Oh, honey! What happened?"

Mollie set her jaw. "Nothing. I just wasn't sure what to bring, so I kept adding things. Be prepared, you know? I may have let it get out of hand, though."

To her mom's credit, she tried to keep her composure, Mollie could see that. But she couldn't help the twitching of her lips or the twinkle of amusement in her eyes. "Being prepared is one thing, but panicking is another. You should have called. I would have come over and helped you pick out what to bring."

She was right. She should have called for backup when she first opened her closet and broke out in a cold sweat. Or at least gone shopping for a new outfit, like Cassie and Jillian had asked her to do. But lately she'd barely had the fortitude to make it through work and school, let alone some kind of girly shopping trip. And asking her mom for packing advice had seemed too close to asking for life advice. Not a door she wanted to open. She'd kept her emotions in check for the last month, but just barely. If her mom started asking her all sorts of questions, she was going to have a breakdown and she absolutely didn't have time for that. "I thought I had it under control."

Her mom checked her watch quickly and then set down her purse. "We've got a few more minutes. Let's see what we can do."

Less than ten minutes later, Mollie watched in bewilderment as her mom easily zipped up the suitcase. Shoes and all. Inside she'd fit three possible outfits for opening night of the show, all better than the ones Mollie had originally put together. And a few pairs of jeans, shirts and underthings. "Mom, you're amazing."

Her mother's cheeks turned a dainty pink. "Thank you, but it was nothing. I've just had a lot more experience packing than you have. When the company I was in traveled, you didn't get much time to get ready, and you were only allowed one bag on the bus. It's a skill you never lose once you learn. Now, grab your stuff and let's hit the road."

Mollie nodded, bending down to give Baby one last hug and kiss before slinging her purse over her shoulder and hefting the suitcase into her hand. Alex would be picking him up to take him to the inn after his shift. The big dog would have a blast playing with Murphy and being loved on by Emma. "I'm right behind you."

They made good time, reaching the outskirts of Orlando in a comfortable silence. Mollie felt herself relax. She'd wanted to drive herself, but the parking costs weren't in her budget. And it was a weekday, which meant Cassie and Jillian were working, as were their husbands. So, she'd asked her mom and prayed it wouldn't turn into an hour-long interrogation session about all the ways she'd messed up her life. So far, so good.

"So, do you have plans with your young man while you're in Atlanta?"

Obviously she'd just been waiting for Mollie to drop her guard.

"His name's Noah, and he's not my young man."

Her mom huffed out a breath while cautiously passing a truck carrying pallets of sod. "Well, I don't know what they're calling it these days. Boyfriend, significant other, partner, whatever. I just assumed you'd be going to see him while you're there. That is where he lives, right?"

Mollie silently counted to ten. *She's only asking because she cares.* "I don't think so. We...we haven't kept in touch, I guess you'd say."

"What? Did you have a fight or something? I know you two didn't have much time together, but he seemed so enamored with you. Your dad and I thought it was all very romantic."

"Maybe, but his ex-girlfriend going into labor with his child was kind of a mood-killer."

"What?" Her mother risked a glance at her before returning her attention to the road.

"Yeah." If they were going to have this conversation, she might as well spill all the details. "He was originally supposed to be in Paradise for his honeymoon." She quickly filled her mother in on the circumstances of the non-marriage and the reason for Noah's proposal.

Her mother's brow furrowed as she processed the convoluted story. "So he tried to do the right thing, even though he wasn't in love with her. I don't agree with that idea, but I can understand his reasoning."

"Right, but then his fiancée ran off a few days before the wedding, leaving him a note saying the baby she was carrying wasn't his. He was heartbroken—about the baby, not her. At least he was until he got a call that she was in labor and it really was his kid."

"Oh, my goodness. I can't imagine how that felt."

Mollie gripped the armrest of the car. "It certainly wasn't the best night of my life. Or his, for that matter."

"So what happened? Did he get back together with the ex? Is that why you broke up?"

She shrugged, purposely looking out the window away from her mother's probing gaze. "I don't know."

"What do you mean, you don't know? He just left and never called or anything?" Indignation laced her tone. Nothing like a man messing with her little girl to bring out the protective mama bear mode.

Mollie felt her face flush. "He did. He sent me a picture of the baby and told me everything was okay. Then I blocked his number."

"You did what?" Her mother took a turn too quickly and had to tap the brakes. "Why would you do something like that?"

"Um, because he has a kid now?"

"And that changes how you feel about him? Did you think he was a virgin or something?"

"Mom! Please." Mollie squirmed in her seat. "I just think he should be focusing on his son right now, not me. And besides, I'm not looking to start a family, so dating a man with a kid isn't in the cards, not now."

"First off, I think you should let him decide what he has time for. But why don't you want a family? You've always been so good with children. All the neighborhood kids always wanted you to be their babysitter."

Her heart panged at the memory. She did love kids, but those were other people's kids. "I am just starting my career. I may have to travel or work long hours. There's really no telling. How can I do that and have a family? You couldn't." That last part slipped out before she could stop it, but maybe a refresher on her mother's own history would make her understand.

"I certainly could have if I'd wanted to. I just didn't want to."

"Because you couldn't do both at the same time, at least not well."

"No. Because I never actually wanted to be a professional dancer, and meeting your father gave me the confidence to finally quit."

Mollie stared at her in shocked silence. Who was

this woman and what had she done with her mother? "You never wanted to be a dancer?" How was that even possible?

"Nope. Your grandmother wanted me to be a ballerina. Dancing was her dream, not mine. Not that I hated it. It was fun at first and I made a lot of wonderful friends. But my feet always hurt, and I was always dieting to try to stay as slender as the other girls. Plus I got horribly homesick whenever we traveled for special shows. When the spot in the New York company opened up, your grandmother just assumed I would go. I almost did. But your father—he reminded me that I was an adult and I needed to make my own decisions. If I wanted to dance, he'd support me. He'd even move to New York to be with me. But if I didn't want to, then I needed to tell my mother, 'Thank you, but no thank you,' and find something I did want to do." A smile crossed her face as she pulled the car into the drop-off line at the terminal.

Despite being firmly strapped in by her seat belt, Mollie's stomach lurched as if it had been tossed by a rogue wave, her childhood view of her mother flipped sideways and backwards. "But what about all the scrapbooks? I thought you kept them because you missed dancing so much."

"Those?" Her mom laughed. "Your grandmother made those. When she died, she left them to me. I only kept them around because you liked looking through them so much. Trust me, I never resented leaving that life behind. I like my life, my family and being able to eat dessert whenever I want. But if I'd wanted to stay, I would have made that work, too. Anything's possible—you just have to want it badly enough. Now give me a kiss and go, or you're going to miss your plane."

Trying to balance a baby on his shoulder while shaving was a skill Noah hadn't quite acquired yet. He had the baby part down—Ryan was happily drooling on the lapels of a starched dress shirt—but the shaving part had ended with a good slice almost taken out of his ear. The intelligent thing to do would have been to put the baby down. He had in fact tried that no fewer than five times in the past hour, and each time his son had scrunched up his face and let loose with blood-curdling wails. Colic, the doctor had said, and it happened like clockwork every evening. From five to nine every night, the little guy needed to be held and walked around, or there was hell to pay. Right now it was six in the evening and Ryan was nothing if not punctual. A habit that would undoubtedly be an asset later in life, but was currently less than helpful.

Wiping off the last of the shaving cream, Noah backtracked to the bedroom and slipped on his shoes. Now to get the baby ready, a process in and of itself. Just leaving the house now took more time and effort than some part-time jobs he'd had. Juggling the baby in one hand and the diaper bag in the other, he headed for what used to be a workspace but was now a makeshift nursery. Inside, the matching crib and changing table jostled for space with a drafting table and shelves full of his sketches. Some of his smaller sculptures were perched on top of the small dresser he'd wedged into the closet, and none of it was properly baby-proofed. Now that the second paternity test had come back positive and the court had officially granted him full custody, he was going to have to find a bigger place. One more thing to put on his growing to-do list.

Hooking the bag on the corner of the changing table, he laid the baby down and swapped out the wet diaper for a dry one as fast as possible, wincing at the inevitable crying. "Sorry, buddy, but this isn't my idea of a good time, either." He maneuvered his son's surprisingly strong legs back into the romper he'd been wearing and checked to be sure the million and one snaps were all fastened. "There, all done."

The crying stopped as soon as he got the baby up on his shoulder again, as if there was some kind of altimeter that alerted Ryan's cry center to changes in altitude. He was just grateful it worked. Next for the bag. Extra diapers, wipes, a change of outfit, a bottle with powdered formula, a thermos of warm water, two pacifiers and his cell phone went in the diaper bag. His wallet and keys went in his pocket, and then he was good to go. Definitely his fastest diaper-to-door time so far. This fatherhood thing was tough, but he was catching on.

He buckled Ryan into his car seat and headed downtown, hoping he wasn't about to make a huge mistake. Up until now, their only outings had been to the pediatrician and the grocery store. An art show was on a whole different level, and quite possibly an awful idea. On the other hand, staying home when Mollie was going to be there showing her work would take more self-control than he had. Which was why he was driving through downtown traffic with a baby crying in the backseat.

In front of the gallery, he checked the car with the valet, then struggled to unsnap the bucket-shaped seat from the car. The thing weighed as much as the baby and was awkward as heck, but if Ryan got sleepy, he'd be more comfortable in it. And trying to steer a stroller around a packed gallery wasn't a challenge he was up for. At least one of them was. Noah was in a cold sweat and he hadn't even made it into the building yet.

Aside from the logistics of carting a newborn through a very formal, very adult event, he had no idea what he was going to say to Mollie when he saw her. *Hey, I know you said you didn't want a family, but any chance you changed your mind?* probably wasn't the best way to lead off. No, he needed to be strong and let her know he was there to support her, not put pressure on her. This might be his only chance with her, and blowing it wasn't an option. Squaring his shoulders, he opened the glass door and walked in.

The gallery itself was one he was familiar with; he'd had a few shows here earlier on in his career. The room was long and narrow, divided into separate viewing areas with cleverly arranged screens. The walls and floor were a nondescript white to better set off the artwork. In contrast, the majority of the people swarming the room were in black, the typical camouflage of the well-to-do Atlanta social scene. Picking one person out of the masses that had shown up for opening night was impossible, but he could feel in his bones that she was here.

The first small area held dozens of photos of bugs. *Insects of the World*, the display tag said. Close-ups of beetles fighting over dung hung next to an incredible shot of a grasshopper in midleap. Intriguing. And not what he was looking for. Pushing past a couple arguing the merits of various photo-editing techniques, he moved through to the next cluster of photographs. These were all of orchids, some potted, some in the wild. He lingered a moment over a particularly colorful one until Ryan tried to take a swipe at it. "No, sir. No sticky baby hands on the merchandise. They'll kick us out for sure, and we haven't found what we came for yet."

Ryan gurgled as if he understood, moving his hand away from the framed picture and sticking it in his mouth. Sucking happily, he rested his head against Noah's chest and despite the chaos around them Noah felt his blood pressure lower. Who'd have thought a baby would be what it took for him to keep his head on straight?

Feeling more grounded, he weaved his way through the crowd, scanning the walls for Mollie's work. He was almost to the back of the building when he saw it and stopped dead in his tracks. There, in a simple wooden frame, was the photo she'd taken of the anhinga the morning they'd gone fishing together. At the time, he'd been so entranced with the photographer he hadn't really noticed the bird. But she had—she'd captured every detail, from the outstretched wings to the sleepy look in its eye. If he didn't know better, he'd have sworn he could reach out and stroke the damp feathers. Standing in front of it he could almost feel the heat of the sun and smell the sea air. It was a tangible piece of Paradise, and a gut-wrenching reminder of the real reason he was here.

Mollie nodded politely as yet another patron asked her about alligators. Blame it on the explosion of nature documentaries or just a severe misunderstanding of geography, but as soon as she mentioned her home state people seemed convinced she must have daily exposure to the reptiles.

"So you've never had one get into your house?" The slightly tipsy blonde took another sip of champagne, her eyes wide at the idea of an alligator infestation.

Mollie resisted the urge to roll her eyes. Tonight was about mingling and being polite. "Nope, they pretty much stay in the water. Just like here. Georgia actually has gators, too, in the southern part of the state."

A vapid nod and the woman moved on, dragging her bored-looking boyfriend towards the bar. Seeing her chance, Mollie limped to the little alcove she'd spotted earlier, between a conference room and the owner's office. The shoes she'd worked so hard to get into the suitcase were torture devices in disguise. Checking that no one was watching, she leaned against the wall and rubbed one aching foot. Wrestling pitbulls for nail trims was easier on the body than an evening in stockings and heels. At least the sequined black dress she'd worn was comfortable, if a bit on the revealing side.

She'd worked the kinks out of one arch and was about to switch feet when the door to the office opened. Great.

So much for her little hiding spot. She slipped her shoe back on and stood up straight. She was already the least experienced photographer in the show; she didn't need to be caught looking like a slacker.

The gallery owner she'd met earlier came out, holding the door for whomever he was speaking with. "It was good to see you again, Mr. James. I hope you enjoy your purchase."

"I'm sure I will. Thank you."

It couldn't be. Mollie's heart skipped a beat, then went into overdrive. He wouldn't have come, not after everything that happened, would he? The voice sounded like him, but the door was blocking her view.

Then it swung closed and he was there. She'd known that he could show up, but she hadn't really believed he would. Otherwise she'd never have had the nerve to come. Seeing him in the flesh had her head spinning and her knees turning to jelly. She grabbed the wall for balance and her wristlet slapped the cement, the noise ringing out in the small alcove.

He turned, and time stopped. For a long moment she just stared, drinking in his presence. He looked a bit thinner, maybe a little tired, but still drop-dead gorgeous. And the man could seriously rock a suit. He looked like a movie star ready for the red carpet, only even more incredible. Because he was Noah.

Noah with a baby in his arms. She shifted her gaze from father to son and was instantly captivated. The little boy was cuter than the picture Noah had sent, with his father's big brown eyes and the sweetest little button nose. "He's wonderful."

"He is. He's also loud, and he has horrible table manners."

She felt a laugh bubble up, all the reasons she'd fallen for this man rising to the surface with it. He was funny and confident and utterly delicious in every way. Why had she pushed him away? There had been reasons, lots of them, but damned if she could think of any now that he was standing in front of her.

Without thinking, she reached out and stroked the baby's curly black hair, loving the silky softness. Her ovaries might actually be exploding right now in the face of so much cuteness. Swallowing hard, she made herself step back. This wasn't her baby, and Noah wasn't her man. She'd had a chance, and she'd blown it. Big time. "I didn't expect to see you here tonight." Not after she'd blocked his calls and ignored him for the last month.

"I said I'd come and I meant it. I know how important it is to you."

She shrugged. "I just figured you'd probably be busy, with the baby and everything."

"What, this guy?" He stroked his son's head. "He loves art galleries. He's a big fan of yours, actually."

She smiled, knowing he'd meant her to. "Right. I should have realized. Well, are you enjoying the show?"

"Yeah, I'd say so. Your stuff is fantastic, by the way."

She felt her cheeks heat. She'd been on the receiving end of dozens of compliments tonight, but his opinion was the one she'd subconsciously needed to hear. "Thanks."

"How about you? Are you enjoying your big night?"

"It's been…exhausting, actually. I think I'm better

at taking pictures than talking about them. I probably ought to head back over there, though, before I'm missed." Not that she wanted to leave him so soon after finding him.

"We'll walk with you."

Walking beside him was like walking back into a dream. Their steps fell into an easy rhythm, just like on their walks on the beach back home. If only they were there now, instead of a room full of pretentious strangers. Too soon they stopped in front of her small display. She pretended to look at the photos she'd seen a thousand times already, anything to keep from looking at him. If she stared too long, she'd lose whatever tiny shred of dignity she had left. No one here wanted to hear her beg him for a second chance.

"That one's my favorite." Oblivious to her discomfort, he moved closer, his arm brushing hers as he pointed to the shot of the anhinga. It was her favorite, too, not because of the composition, but because it was a memento of a nearly perfect day. "In fact, I just bought it."

"You bought it? You didn't have to do that. I would have given you a copy if you'd asked."

"Hey, I have to do my part to support the arts, right? And it would have been kind of hard to ask, given how well you've been avoiding my phone calls."

Ugh. "I know, I'm sorry. I just thought, well, I thought that you needed to have some time to focus on your son. I didn't mean to—"

"Mollie, it's fine." He rested a hand on her shoulder, bared by the halter top of her dress. "I understand, and honestly, you were probably right to do it. I've had to make a lot of adjustments and rethink a lot of things."

Things like his relationship with his ex? The only way to find out was to ask. "Sounds tough. Have you been able to come to some sort of understanding with Angela after everything that happened?"

His jaw tensed, and he looked suddenly looked much wearier than he had a few minutes ago. "I guess you could say that."

An awful thought popped into her head. "Is she here with you tonight?" There was no way she could handle seeing the happy family together. Petty or not, she would rather wrestle one of the alligators people kept asking her about than make small talk with that woman.

"No, she's not with me. Not tonight, not any night."

Was it wrong to feel relieved? Because that was definitely the emotion sweeping over her. And right behind it was concern. "I'm sorry. Is she giving you any trouble as far as visitation goes?"

He looked down at the baby on his chest. "None. She gave me full custody."

Wait, what? "What do you mean, full custody?"

"I mean he's mine, full-time. Angela decided she wasn't ready to be a mother, so she gave me full custody, then took off again. Her new boyfriend has a fancy job on Wall Street and she's not letting him or his money out of her sight."

Mollie felt her mouth drop open. "She chose some new guy over her own child? Who does that? What kind of woman could walk out on her kid like that?"

"I wish I could explain it, but all I can say is that

Angela isn't like most women. She's wired differently, I guess, and if she wasn't up to being a parent, well, at least she was honest about it. This was probably the most selfless thing she's ever done, although I doubt she realizes it."

"So you've been taking care of him all on your own?"

"Not entirely. My parents have helped a lot, actually. Having a grandchild around seems to have helped heal some old wounds. We're probably closer now than we've ever been."

"That sounds nice." She smacked herself on the head. "I mean it's nice that your parents are helping you. Not that she took off."

He smiled and reached out and stroked a stray hair off her forehead, then quickly moved his hand back to his side. "I know what you meant, and it is nice, actually. And as hard as it's been, adjusting to being a father, it's also been pretty great."

"I bet it has. Angela's a fool to give him up."

"Well, not every woman wants to be a mother."

She sucked in a breath at implication. "That was a low blow, Noah. There's a big difference between choosing not to have children and walking out on one."

Noah couldn't believe he'd said that. "Damn it, I didn't mean it that way. Trust me, you are nothing like her."

She seemed to be considering his apology, but an earsplitting wail kept her from replying, proving once again that babies had no sense of timing. "Sorry, he's probably hungry. I need to find somewhere quiet and feed him before he gets any crankier."

Her eyes widened. "He gets worse than this?"

"You have no idea." Ryan could put a siren to shame once he got going. Even the nurses at the hospital had been impressed.

"There's a small meeting room in the back. Will that work?"

He nodded and started walking, moving quickly. There was no point in trying to talk over the baby's cries, which were already inciting some hostile looks. He'd been lucky Ryan had kept quiet for so long, probably distracted from his usual nighttime antics by all the people and artwork. Mollie pushed open a wood and glass door and led him into a small but serviceable conference room. A round table took up the majority of the space, with six comfortable-looking chairs spaced evenly around it. Dropping into one, he dug into a black, messenger-style diaper bag with one hand while balancing the baby in his lap with the other.

"Need a hand?"

"You don't mind holding him for a second?"

"I wouldn't have offered if I did. Here, hand him over." She reached out and Noah found himself placing the baby in her arms.

"Be careful of his—"

"Head? Yeah, I know. Believe it or not, I've done this before." She bounced lightly on her toes, calming Ryan's cries. "At one point, I was the most sought-after babysitter on Paradise Isle."

"I can believe it." She'd certainly worked her magic

on his son, who was now watching her in wide-eyed fascination. It seemed she now had both of the James men under her spell. Mixing the powdered formula with the water from the thermos, he made up the bottle quickly, handing it over when she reached for it.

"Here we go big guy, dinnertime." Ryan latched on to the bottle nipple and greedily started suckling.

Captivated, Noah watched Mollie feed his son, not wanting to spoil the moment with small talk. Angela might not have been up to motherhood, but Mollie was obviously a natural. Finally the bottle was empty, and without missing a beat she grabbed a clean cloth from the bag and tossed it over her shoulder before shifting the baby to burp him.

"Okay, I give. You're obviously an expert at this. I'd have pegged you for a total baby lover if I didn't know better."

"I never said I don't like babies. Or kids. But being a parent is a whole lot more than just liking babies. It's about sacrifice and putting their needs before your own."

"You're right, I'm sorry. I promise I didn't come here to try to pressure you into anything."

"Why are you here, Noah? After everything I said in Paradise, and then shutting you out after Ryan was born, what made you come here tonight?" He could hear the sincerity in her voice; she wasn't fishing for a compliment or trying to corner him into anything. She really didn't know.

"I came because I couldn't stay away." There it was, the bare truth. "I know I should leave you alone—I'm a single dad, and you aren't ready for a family. And I want you to follow your dreams and do all the amazing things you want to do. You've got a path you want to take, and I promise, I'm not going to stand in your way."

"I know you aren't."

He let out a sigh of relief. At least he hadn't ruined things, not yet. She was still listening, her eyes on his as she rested her cheek on his son's head. If he could freeze time and capture this moment forever, he would. But then he'd be doing exactly what he'd promised not to do. He couldn't control her or keep her in his life, not matter how much he wanted to. "What I'm trying to say is, I've waited a lifetime to find the perfect woman, and a few more years won't kill me. All I'm asking is that if you ever do decide to try your hand at having a family, you give me a call. I'm willing to wait as long as it takes."

Tears filled her big brown eyes and spilled down her cheeks, landing in his son's dark curls. He wiped one away with his thumb, loving how she leaned into his touch. "Don't cry. You don't have to promise anything. I shouldn't have even asked. I just thought if there was some hope, it would make it easier to be apart. But that's not fair to you. Let's just forget I said anything, okay? This is your big night and I've got you burping a baby in the back room." He moved to take his son. "I'll take him, and you go mingle while you can."

Instead of handing the sleepy baby over, she held on, shaking her head even as she smiled. "No way. You can't make me go back out there. Besides, you had your chance to talk. Now it's my turn."

* * *

Mollie couldn't decide if she wanted to laugh or cry, but either might wake the baby sleeping so peacefully in her arms. So she took a deep breath and just went for it. "I don't want you to wait." He started to speak and she cut him off, needing him to hear this. "I don't want you to wait because I don't want to wait."

"You don't?" Noah looked so startled she ended up laughing after all, unable to contain the happiness welling up inside her.

"No. This past month has been a nightmare. I miss you constantly, and I'm tired of that. It sucks."

The corner up of mouth tipped up in a lopsided grin. "You missed me."

"Yes, I just said that. And I hated it. Hell, even Baby missed you. So we have to figure something out."

"But what about your career? Your dreams? As well as the show went tonight, I'm sure you're going to have all sorts of opportunities opening up. I think there was even a magazine editor checking out your stuff."

"Seriously? An editor? That would be amazing."

"It would. But it also means you're going to have to make some big decisions. If she doesn't contact you, I'm sure others will. You're going to have lots of work if you want it, mark my words. And as much of a rush as I know that is, it can be overwhelming, too."

"All the more reason I'm going to need your support. I don't want to do this without you. I realized that on the way here. I've been worried about messing up my career with a relationship, afraid I'd look back one day and wonder what might have been. But Noah, the one thing I know I'd regret would be losing you, letting go of whatever we have going on here. And that's scarier than anything I can think of."

"So what are you saying?" He stepped closer, the baby the only thing between them. "What is it you want?"

"Everything." Stretching onto her toes, she ran her free hand over his jaw, feeling the stubble his razor had missed. "You, a career, I want it all."

He leaned in, his mouth inches away, close enough for her to smell his cologne over the sweet scent of baby shampoo and powder. "And what about Ryan? I'm not asking you to be his mother, but he and I are kind of a package deal now."

"Even better." She pressed her lips to his in a gentle kiss. "In case you hadn't noticed, he and I get along just fine." Better than fine. She could feel herself falling for the little guy already as he slept on her shoulder. It probably shouldn't be a surprise, given how fast his father had slipped past her defenses.

"I can see that. But right now, he's kind of in the way." Noah gently pulled the baby out of her arms and lowered him into the car seat, buckling it around him. "There, now, where were we?"

"I'm not sure," she teased. "Maybe you should remind me."

"Maybe I should." He cupped her bare shoulders with his hands, then ran them ever so slowly down her body to rest on her hips. "By the way, this dress should be illegal. I think my blood pressure hit dangerous levels when I turned around and saw you in it." He pulled her against him, and bent his mouth to her ear. "I'm still feeling a bit woozy. I might even need mouth to mouth."

Goose bumps rose where his breath tickled her skin. "I think that could be arranged. Better safe than sorry." She turned her head and kissed him then, needing him more than she needed her next breath. His lips tasted like champagne, his tongue like velvet, exploring her as if they had all the time in the world. Tangling her hands in his hair, she wondered how she had ever thought she could walk away from him. "I missed this especially," she murmured against his lips. "I don't ever want to stop."

He sucked her bottom lip between his teeth, nipping lightly before letting go. "Then don't. Let's spend the rest of our lives doing this."

Her heart skittered out of rhythm. "Are you... Did you just ask me...?" No, he couldn't have meant that.

He pulled back just enough to look her in the eyes, amusement crinkling his at the corners. "Was I asking you to marry me? Honestly, I don't know. Isn't it too soon for that?"

Butterflies swarmed in her stomach. "Probably. Maybe."

His hands tightened on her waist. "What would you have said if I had?"

"Oh, no, you don't. It doesn't work that way. If you want an answer, you have to ask. Properly."

His mouth was firm, but she saw twinkle of a smile in his eyes. Without letting go of her, he lowered himself onto one knee. Behind him the baby was still sleeping, oblivious to the anticipation flooding the room. "So help me, if you're about to turn me down—"

"Hurry up, before the baby wakes up."

He rolled his eyes. "I thought you wanted this done properly?"

"I do, but I'm also impatient."

"So it seems." He cleared his throat and reached up to take her hands in his. "Mollie Post, I'm probably exactly the wrong thing for you in so many ways, but I promise to spend my life making yours better, if you'll let me. Would you do me the honor of being my wife?"

She smiled, the tears falling for real now. "I've always wanted adventure and excitement, and I thought that meant traveling the world, reaching new goals. But Noah, nothing could be more of an adventure than creating a life with you and Ryan."

He cocked his head, looking up at her from the floor. "That means yes, right?"

"Yes."

Chapter Nine

Mollie grabbed another box full of odds and ends off the garage floor and hauled it over to the backyard table where she had been sorting since breakfast. It was nearing noon now and she'd barely made a dent. "Are you sure you don't want to just rent some studio space somewhere?" In the month since he'd proposed, she'd floated the idea several times, but he'd turned her down each time.

Noah looked up from the workbench he was building. "I'm not going to rent space just so you don't have to clean out the garage. There's plenty of space for your photography equipment and my tools, and I'd rather work from home so I can see Ryan more."

"Fine." He was right; there was plenty of room in her home, or at least there would be once she finished going through all this stuff. So far she'd found everything from her third-grade report card to a tangle of rusted fishing hooks, not to mention the old magazines that were slowly turning to dust. Why had she kept all this stuff? "But I hate you for making me do this."

"No, you don't. You love me."

She sighed in annoyance. "Yeah, I do. But I'd still rather be on the beach, or fishing, or doing anything else, pretty much." She wiped the sweat from her forehead. It was a perfect summer day for the beach, but way too hot to be working outside.

"Anything, huh?" Noah waggled his eyebrows at her. "I might be amenable to a break, depending on what activity you had in mind."

She felt her face heat, and not just from the blazing sun overhead. "Not in front of the baby." Ryan was in his swing a few feet away, Baby curled up on the ground beside him. Both were snoozing in the shade of the big oak tree and not paying any attention to Noah's suggestive comments. "Besides, it's only a few more days."

"Three days. Three very long days," he muttered, attacking the sanding with more vigor than was probably necessary.

She felt a moment of guilt, but then he winked at her, and everything was okay. She knew it was silly, but superstitious or not, she wanted her and Noah's wedding to be totally different from the one he'd planned with Angela. Up to and including waiting until after the ceremony for sex. He'd grumbled, but finally agreed, warning her that she'd better be prepared for a *vigorous* honeymoon. As if he was the only one who was impatient. Even now, the sight of him shirtless, glistening with sweat while he worked had her wanting to ambush him right there on top of the table he was building. No, he certainly wasn't the only one fighting their urges. But it would be worth it on their wedding night.

Speaking of which. "Did your parents' flight get in okay?"

He nodded, not breaking his rhythm as he worked. "Yup, they sent me a text saying they were on their way to the Sandpiper and are looking forward to the rehearsal dinner tonight."

"Good." His father still made her a bit nervous with his military demeanor, but Noah's mom kept him in check and was turning out to be a wonderful friend. They'd spent quite a bit of time together in Atlanta when Mollie had flown up to go apartment-hunting with Noah. He'd offered to move full time to Paradise, but in the end they'd decided to keep a place in both cities. That way they could go back and forth as they pleased, and Ryan could spend time with all of his grandparents, of which he had an abundance. Mollie's parents were totally in love with the little guy, and of course Noah's parents had been a huge help since day one. Even Angela's parents had made cautious inroads, not wanting to miss out on their grandchild's life despite their daughter's decision.

Yes, Ryan was loved, but that wasn't a surprise. He was as sweet a baby as she'd ever seen; he'd even gotten over his colic after a formula switch. And although nature photography was still her focus, taking pictures of the newborn was quickly becoming an addiction. It helped that he seemed just enamored with her as she was with him, often reaching for her even when Noah was there. And as much as she'd worried that having a relationship or a baby would stifle her career, she'd actually been spending more time behind the camera than ever and had even signed a contract with a state-wide magazine for some of her photos.

The only slight regret she had was leaving her job at the animal clinic. It was hard not seeing Cassie and Jillian every day, but now she could double up on her classes and graduate next spring. Living off of Noah's money was a bit disconcerting, but he'd blown off her concerns, saying it was an investment in their future. But she, or rather her parents, had drawn the line at paying for the wedding. They'd been saving for years for a day they'd thought might never come and weren't going to be denied the privilege of orchestrating the big event.

Mollie had asked for a simple ceremony on the beach, but her mom was nearly unstoppable. The final compromise was a ceremony on the beach, with a huge reception afterward back at the Sandpiper. The tents had been rented, flowers and food ordered, musicians hired, and now all that was left was to actually say "I do."

And it couldn't happen soon enough.

Noah stood barefoot in the office of the Sandpiper and pulled at the too-tight collar of his shirt. He'd ordered the white linen shirt and pants online, and everything fit but the neck. He somehow hadn't noticed that when he'd tried it on the day it arrived and now it was too late to do anything about it. Giving up, he undid the top button and hoped Mollie wouldn't mind. She'd wanted a casual, nontraditional wedding—one undone collar shouldn't be a huge deal. Should it?

"Does this look okay?"

Alex, Cassie's husband, shook his head. "Sorry, I don't answer fashion questions, not about suits and stuff. This is the most dressed up I've been since my own wedding." Alex gestured to the khaki slacks and blue, short-sleeved dress shirt he and Nic, the other groomsman, were wearing. "But if I was going to say anything, it would be to relax. She's not going to ditch you at the altar because your collar's unbuttoned."

Noah swallowed hard.

"Oops, sorry, man. I wasn't thinking. But seriously, Mollie's not Angela. If she didn't want to marry you, she would have told your sorry butt no when you first asked her."

"Good point." Mollie didn't say things she didn't mean, and she didn't play games. She was exactly what he wanted in a woman, which was why he was having such a hard time believing this was real. Just a few short months ago, he'd been a loner who spent more time with a blow torch than with other humans. Now he was surrounded by family and newfound friends. He had a new connection with his parents, was raising a son, and in a matter of minutes he'd have the perfect wife to share it all with. It would have been less shocking to win the lottery while being struck by lightning.

A knock at the door was followed by a mad dash into the room by Emma, Alex and Cassie's nearly five-year-old daughter. A few seconds behind her was Cassie, looking flustered but beautiful in the baby blue maternity dress Mollie had chosen for her two pregnant bridesmaids. "Sorry, she insisted she needed to show Alex her dress. Again. I'm raising a fashionista here."

Alex admired Emma as she twirled in her flower-girl dress and then swept her up for a hug. "Nah, she's just a daddy's girl, aren't you, sweetheart?" Emma nodded, all dimples and curls. "Probably was pining away for me."

Cassie rolled her eyes. "She saw you at lunch." But she was smiling, too, obviously pleased by the close relationship the two had forged. Alex wasn't Emma's biological father, but you wouldn't know it from the way they acted. Funny how that worked. Love trumped biology with them, just as it did with Mollie and Ryan. Somehow the right people had found each other, against all the odds.

The door opened again, this time for Alex's father. "They're all set, son. Let's get this show on the road."

"Mommy, it's time! I have to go get my flowers!" Emma scrambled out of Alex's lap, her devotion to her father paling in comparison to flower-girl duties.

"Okay, let's go." Cassie blew her husband a kiss, then let Emma pull her out the door.

"Where's Nic? He was supposed to meet us in here." Noah hadn't seen his other groomsman since they'd first gotten to the inn a few hours ago.

"I just saw him," his father assured him. "He was helping the musicians get set up, something about having to reinforce the bandstand to support the weight. He was going to run and wash up, then meet us out back."

Noah shook his head. Nic had gone from power suits

and boardroom meetings to hammering nails and washing dishes, and seemed perfectly happy about it. But then, life was full of twists and turns, wasn't it?

Together the three men trooped down the hall and out the back door, where they found Nic waiting for them. The back porch had been transformed into a buffet line, where uniformed caterers were setting out an ample spread of summer fare. Down on the lawn, tables had been set up under a tent, with large fans to supplement the sea breeze. And of course there was the bandstand and the dance floor that Nic had built himself.

But that was all for later. First he had to get through the ceremony. The men took the steps down to the beach, where the minister waited under an arbor made from driftwood. Behind it was the ever-changing backdrop of the sea, and although the sun hadn't quite set, a glimmer of a moon could be seen peeking over the horizon.

Taking his place beside the minister, he felt his earlier anxiety ease. Something about the enduring sound of the waves steadied him, that and the people he was now facing, all of them here to show their support. He'd come to Paradise to heal his wounds and found so much more.

The first strains of the wedding march caught his attention, and the crowd turned as one to see the bridal party make its way down the aisle. First Jillian, looking radiant, then Cassie, and then little Emma with her flower basket. After all the petals had been thrown, enthusiastically if not gracefully, the music changed again, and Noah felt his heart skip a beat.

There, at the far end of aisle, was Mollie, and she was the most beautiful thing he'd ever seen. Her simple strapless dress was perfect, no lace or flounces for her. No, she was simple and open and honest, and he was about to be the happiest man in the world.

Mollie made her way through the sand, trying to focus on Noah's face and not the countless people staring at her. Somehow she'd forgotten that she'd be so on display, and it was just short of terrifying. What if she tripped? Or what if people thought her dress was too short or too casual? The sheath had seemed perfect back in Jillian's bedroom a few minutes ago, but maybe she should have worn something more traditional. Panic, an unfamiliar and unwelcome feeling, clawed at her, stifling her.

Her father patted her arm where it was looped through his in a show of reassurance, but her lungs still refused to work properly, and she was practically hyperventilating by the time they reached the front row of seats where her and Noah's families sat.

Little Ryan was in his grandmother's lap, and he cried out as Mollie passed, stretching his pudgy arms towards her. Noah's mom flushed and tried to shush him, but the little boy just cried harder, his face turning red.

Jolted out of her self-induced panic, Mollie stopped and stepped away from her father, moving to take the little boy. "You're right, little man," she reassured him, snugging him to her chest. "You deserve to be up there, too."

Linking her arm back with her father's, she let him take her and Ryan the rest of the way. Somehow the people behind her didn't matter now, not with Noah at her side and Ryan in her arms. She was able to smile and enjoy the rest of the ceremony, and then, so much faster than she'd expected, they were married.

She quickly passed Ryan back to his grandmother, and then she was walking back down the aisle—this time, arm in arm with her new husband. Squeezing her hand, Noah leaned down to whisper in her ear. "You look incredible in that dress, but I'm dying to peel it off of you."

She shivered in anticipation. "You don't look bad yourself." In fact, he looked amazing. The summery white fabric made him look even more dark and handsome, and she knew the loose material hid some seriously hard muscles. "I say we make a quick appearance and then start the honeymoon early."

"It's a deal."

An hour and a half later, it was clear that making an appearance took a lot longer than expected when there were so many people to greet. And both sets of parents had insisted that the bride and groom couldn't leave until after the cake cutting at the very earliest. Which, the caterer had told her, wasn't supposed to happen for another forty-five minutes. Well, that just wasn't going to work for her. She'd talked to everyone she needed to talk to, she'd had an amazing first dance in the arms of her groom, she'd stuffed herself silly with crab cakes and fruit and, darn it, she was done.

Time to take matters into her own hands. Putting

down her champagne glass on the nearest table, she scanned the tent for Noah. Not seeing him or Ryan, she cut across the yard where Baby, Murphy and Alex's K9 partner, Rex, were chewing on celebratory dog bones, giving them a pat before climbing the porch steps on the side of the house. Here, some of the older guests had gathered, preferring the Sandpiper's comfortable patio furniture to the folding chairs on the lawn. Noah was there, too, talking to his mother, baby Ryan asleep in the portable swing. Perfect.

"Sorry to interrupt, just need to steal my husband away for a minute." She grabbed Noah's arm and tugged. "Mama James, you don't mind keeping an eye on Ryan, do you?"

"Of course not, dear. I'm having a lovely chat with the ladies I've met. You two go enjoy the party."

Oh, she planned on it. Tugging Noah with her, she took him down the stairs and then, making sure none of the women on the patio were watching, around the building and down a well-mulched path.

"Where on earth are you taking me?"

"Somewhere we can be alone." She pointed to the brick and timber house at the end of the path. "Jillian said the house is finished, and as soon as they furnish it they'll move in."

"Are you serious?"

She pulled on their joined hands, swinging him toward her for a hard, fast kiss. "Like a heart attack."

She took the steps to the front door two at a time, sliding a key from where she'd hidden it in her cleavage.

"Where on earth did you get a key to Jillian and Nic's house?"

She rolled her eyes. "Jillian gave it to me. She knew I'd insisted we wait until we were married and since they won't be moving in for another month, she figured we might want to get a jump on things, so to speak."

Noah stopped in his tracks. "Isn't consummating our marriage in your friend's half-built house a bit... unorthodox?"

"Honey, if you wanted traditional, you married the wrong girl. Now, are you coming or not?"

Noah followed her in, and she locked the door behind him, laying the key on the windowsill before closing the blinds. Turning towards him, her heart pounding, she unzipped her dress in one swift move, letting it fall to the floor. Noah's draw dropped, and she had to stifle a giggle at his shock.

"You weren't wearing anything under your dress."

"Nope."

"You do realize, if I'd known that, we probably wouldn't have even made it through the vows." He stepped closer, his eyes dark with lust, but she saw love there as well, and her own need increased in response.

"Well, then, Mr. James, now you know. So I suggest you get those clothes off and we make this marriage official."

Growling his response, he tore his shirt off, sending buttons flying.

"Noah, your shirt! We still have to go back for the cake cutting."

"I'll borrow one from Nic. Or go naked, I don't

care." He kicked off the rest of his clothes, and she got a glimpse of his perfect body before he was picking her up and carrying her to down the hall.

"Where are we going?" Dizzy, she closed her eyes, and let her other senses take control.

"Whatever room has carpet."

Noah couldn't believe Mollie had set this up, even so far as stashing a box of condoms on the mantel, but he wasn't going to argue. He'd been taking cold showers for too long to turn her down now. But he was too primed to go slow, and hardwood floors might leave them both bruised. The back bedroom had the plush carpet he was looking for. Dropping to his knees, he laid her out in front of him. She was gorgeous, and she was his.

"You know I planned for this to be special, with candles and flower petals and music," hc muttered against her neck, loving how she squirmed as he kissed her there.

"I couldn't wait for special," she whimpered, her breathing fast and shallow. "I need you, Noah."

"I need you, too." That was the truth, and with a quick motion of his hips, he gave her all of himself, joining them together the way man and woman had joined since the beginning of time. It wasn't the slow and gentle lovemaking he'd envisioned for their wedding night, but it was raw and honest and real, just like the woman beneath him. He kept his eyes open, watching her fall apart before finding his own release inside her. Panting, he dropped down, rolling off of her when she feebly pushed at him.

"That was incredible." Mollie snuggled up beside him, her hand making circles of gooseflesh on his chest. "We should do that again. A lot."

"Agreed. But as much as I'd like to lie here with you all night, we need to get back for the whole cake thing."

Her hand dropped lower, and his breath caught. "Actually, I was thinking. If we were just a little late, that would probably be fine. It's not like they can start without us, right?"

He rolled her on top of him, unable to resist her logic. Or her body. "Smart *and* sexy—I knew I married you for a reason. Hell, they can keep their cake, I've got everything I want right here."

* * * * *

Don't miss the previous installments in
Katie Meyer's PARADISE ANIMAL CLINIC *series,*
THE PUPPY PROPOSAL and
A VALENTINE FOR THE VETERINARIAN,
available now wherever
Harlequin books and ebooks are sold.

COMING NEXT MONTH FROM

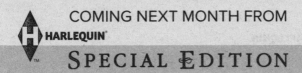 **HARLEQUIN®**

SPECIAL EDITION

Available May 24, 2016

#2479 WED BY FORTUNE
The Fortunes of Texas: All Fortune's Children
by Judy Duarte
When pregnant single mom Sasha-Marie Gibault returns home to lick her wounds, she reconnects with her childhood crush, Graham Robinson. But the rancher's interest in this little family is jeopardized when they learn he may really be a famous Fortune.

#2480 HIS DESTINY BRIDE
Welcome to Destiny
by Christyne Butler
The one time responsible Katie Ledbetter throws caution to the wind, she winds up pregnant after one night of passion. Her child's father, gorgeous Nolan Murphy, wants Katie and their baby in his life. But is the single dad ready to give love and family a second shot?

#2481 HIGH COUNTRY BABY
The Brands of Montana
by Joanna Sims
Rough-and-tumble bull rider Clint McAllister loves taking risks, like seducing Taylor Brand. When Taylor suggests that he get her pregnant, she has Clint shouting "Whoa!" But a lifelong trail ride with a wife and child might just be what the cowboy ordered.

#2482 LUCY & THE LIEUTENANT
The Cedar River Cowboys
by Helen Lacey
Back home from war, ex-soldier Brant Parker wants nothing more than to bury his grief in his work. Dr. Lucy Monero, who's loved him since childhood, is determined to keep the loner afloat—and make him hers!

#2483 FROM GOOD GUY TO GROOM
The Colorado Fosters
by Tracy Madison
Scarred from the inside out after a tragic accident, Andi Caputo seeks healing in Steamboat Springs, Colorado. Her physical therapist, Ryan Bradshaw, is drawn to his lovely new patient, but can he be the hero that Andi needs—forever?

#2484 THE FIREFIGHTER'S FAMILY SECRET
The Barlow Brothers
by Shirley Jump
While trying to repent for a past accident, Colton Barlow is shaken when he learns of his long-lost family in Stone Gap. Rachel Morris tempts him to stay in town, but how can he give her his heart when he's not sure who he really is anymore?

YOU CAN FIND MORE INFORMATION ON UPCOMING HARLEQUIN® TITLES, FREE EXCERPTS AND MORE AT WWW.HARLEQUIN.COM.

HSECNM0516

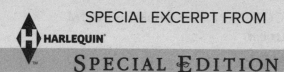
"I'm so proud of the woman you've become." He trailed his fingers along her upper arm, setting off a rush of tingles that nearly unraveled her at the seams.

What was going on? Why had he touched her like that? Did she dare read something into it?

The emotion glowing in his eyes warmed her heart in such an unexpected way that she forgot her momentary concern and pretended, just for a moment, that something romantic was brewing between them.

She tossed him a playful grin. "I'm glad to hear you say that, especially when you once thought of me as a pest."

"Yeah, well, I wish I'd known then who the woman that little girl was going to grow up to be. Things might have been…"

His words drifted off, but her heart soared at the

implication. Their gazes locked until he pulled his hand away and muttered, "Dammit."

"What's the matter?" she asked, although she feared what he might say.

"This is a real struggle for me, Sasha."

She had a wild thought that he actually might be attracted to her and waited to hear him out, bracing herself for disappointment.

He merely studied her as if she ought to know just what he was talking about. But she'd be darned if she'd read something nonexistent into it.

Graham raked his fingers through his hair. "I'm feeling things for you that I have no right to feel," he admitted.

"Seriously?"

"I'm afraid so. And I'm sorry, especially since you still belong to another man."

Sasha hadn't "belonged" to anyone in a long time, and if truth be told, the only man she wanted to belong to was Graham.

Don't miss
WED BY FORTUNE
by USA TODAY bestselling author Judy Duarte,
available June 2016 wherever
Harlequin® Special Edition books and ebooks are sold.

www.Harlequin.com

Love the Harlequin book you just read?

Your opinion matters.

Review this book on your favorite book site, review site, blog or your own social media properties and share your opinion with other readers!

Be sure to connect with us at:
Harlequin.com/Newsletters
Facebook.com/HarlequinBooks
Twitter.com/HarlequinBooks